Whisper of Elves

(Elves, Drelves & Dragons: Book Two)

C. Star

Join my mailing list to receive the latest news about my books (and extra goodies!)

Community:

Mail: Cynastar019@gmail.com

My Website: Cstarbooks.com

Signup for Newsletter:

https://cstarbooks.com/#newsletter

Thank you for reading my books!

www.Cstarbooks.com

Dedication

Dedicated to Karen N.

Thank you for encouraging me on this fantastical journey!
You, like Finnian, are a true and loyal friend,
and I am blessed to know you.

Don't miss Book One of Elves, Drelves & Dragons!

Table of Contents

The three Realms
Drelf Kingdom
Dragon Graveyard
Larimar Falls
Shrouded Vale
The Arden
Elf Kingdom
Rivenmoor
Fae Bridge
Dragon Kingdom

Prologue

Long before memory — before the realms were divided by flame and shadow — there was balance.

Elves and dragons walked in accord beneath the Great Covenant: a bond forged in honor, sealed in trust. Together, they guarded the boundaries between sky and soil, fire and forest.

In those days, all dragons were white — beacons of light, bearers of balance and peace.

But pride breeds deceit.

And where light burns brightest, shadow waits to follow.

One dragon, consumed by envy, fell into darkness. His once-brilliant scales turned black as night, and shadow claimed his heart. He conceived a lie to take what was never his to claim.

Cloaked in white flame, he wore the guise of purity, his scales gleaming with false light. The elves, blinded by beauty and faith, did not see the darkness beneath.

One of their own — a maiden of great renown — was deceived by the illusion and bound herself to him.

From that union was born the first drelf.

To the elves, she was heresy made flesh — proof that dragon fire had corrupted their blood.

To the dragons, she was a failure — a mingling that defied their creed of pure lineage.

And so, both realms turned upon her.

The Great Covenant shattered.

Trust burned to ash.

And the drelf — born of both light and fire — was cast into exile, bound to neither realm, despised by both.

In the wake of that betrayal, more dragons turned inward and darkened, their once-white scales consumed by corruption.

Balance faltered.

And from that broken bond rose Vartharax, the dark dragon lord — and at his side, his right hand of shadow, Drakor. Small by dragon standards, twisted in body but sharp of mind, Drakor used cunning where strength failed him; wit over wing, guile over flame, turning intellect into a weapon.

Together they bent ancient magic to their will, corrupting flame into darkness and oath into deceit.

And they swore that nothing would ever mend what they had broken.

Yet even as the Covenant fell, the white dragons — keepers of balance and light — foresaw what was to come.

They gathered in secret and forged a prophecy in flame and song:

That when the realms again stood upon the edge of ruin, marks of power would rise born from the bloodlines of those once divided.

Through them, the balance could be restored… or lost forever.

It was not a promise. It was a warning.

A test woven into — that when darkness rose again, choice would decide what strength could not.

And prophecies are not so easily silenced.

The first mark has already awakened — burned upon a drelf, descendant of the outcast line.

From that spark of forbidden blood, light has risen again.

Its power ripples through the realms, turning the tide toward hope.

Toward the elves. Toward the drelves.

For the first time in an age, the balance leans toward the light.

Yet balance is never still.

Now, a second mark stirs.

Not of peace. Not of unity.

But of power — true power.

Enough to strengthen the light and drive back the dark.

Or, if it falls into the wrong hands… enough to drown the realms in shadow once more.

It pulses, faint and unclaimed, hidden behind laughter and loss —

waiting for the moment it will burn through flesh and fate alike.

Not in fire. Not in glory.

But in silence.

The storm has passed, yet its echo has only just begun.

The realms — still fractured, still bleeding — do not yet feel the weight of what is rising.

Not the battle-worn elves tending to their wounded.

Not the dragons buried beneath ash and ruin.

Not the drelves kneeling beside their dead.

Not even the one who bears it.

Especially not them.

But the darkness feels it.

It knows the pattern.

It has waited before — and it will not wait again.

And far beneath the world, where flame and shadow twine,

The mark stirs, waiting to be claimed.

Previously, in Mark of Elves…

Fizzlewing's eyes twinkled again, mischief layered with truth. "We must find the bearer of the second mark. Before the darkness does."

Finnian exhaled sharply, muttering under it. "Bloody elves. There's another mark?"

Lightning cracked above, cleaving through the stillness like a warning. The heavens trembled.

Far above—veiled at the center of the storm—wings carved through the darkness, and eyes of fire blazed.

Still watching.

Still waiting.

And somewhere far away, deep in the Elven wilds, a second mark stirred to life—oblivious of the tempest it would bring.

Chapter 1

Lyria's pulse hammered, her hand flying to the mark on her throat.

It burned — alive, demanding — just as it had the day it appeared.

A curse.

To her. To her drelf kingdom. To the elves.

And now… to another.

The mark held power — ancient, dangerous, coveted. Power that could heal or destroy, depending on who claimed it.

She had been hunted for that power ever since.

First by the nemods—creatures of darkness and shadow—sent by their master, Drakor, the twisted dragon who served the will of something far older and crueler: the dark dragon lord, Vartharax.

Then by shadow panthers and wyverns—unleashed to hunt beside them, swift and merciless in their pursuit.

Fizzlewing's words echoed in her mind: *"We must find the bearer of the second mark. Before the darkness does."*

She knew what that darkness felt like.

What it smelled like.

What it *sounded* like…

The roar of wings.

The stench of smoke and blood.

Flame splitting the sky as Drakor descended, his shadow swallowing the light.

Eldrin's eyes—pleading, lost in the chaos.

Grasping. Slipping. Falling.

The flash of her blade, slashing through the bandages that bound her broken wing.

The sear of heat as she dove into the abyss after him.

Then—light.

And the white dragon's voice, deep and echoing through her soul:

"The choice was made."

It was that choice—the moment a drelf risked her life for an elf—that released the power of the mark.

Enough to break the darkness and save them all.

For the moment.

The battle is over.

But the war had only shifted.

Another mark?

Lyria gasped, stumbling as Eldrin's hand caught her arm. The scent of ash still clung to her skin, though the fires had died. The mark pulsed beneath her fingers—a heartbeat that wasn't her own.

Her kingdom lay in ruins. The dead needed burying. The wounded, tending. And the elves—the same elves who had once banished her kind—now stood in her city's shadow, waiting to see if the fragile truce would hold.

And now they had to find a second mark… before the darkness did?

The weight pressed upon her like an anvil. Her breath came in shallow gasps as she surveyed what remained of the battlefield. Smoke clung to the air, thick and metallic, mingling with the sharp tang of ash and blood.

Her gaze drifted across the ruin, overwhelmed by what she saw. How would they ever recover? She searched for something… someone to steady her.

Eldrin was her first thought. The elf who had saved her in the Enchanted Forest when the nemods closed in, and her strength was nearly gone. He was the one who pulled her through the portal into the Elven kingdom—who carried her bleeding body through enemy paths to the healer's door, risking treason against his own father, King Eldermyst. And now, he stood beside her in the aftermath.

Then there was Gantar—the elven sage and healer—standing with staff in hand; his silver hair streaked with soot. His eyes found hers, steady and searching.

He, too, had risked everything. For her. For Eldrin. For the prophecy. When Eldrin had knocked at his door—soaked in rain, his tunic torn and stained with her blue-green blood—Gantar had hidden her beneath his own roof, tended her wounds, and sent them both to the Shrouded Vale when danger closed in. For that mercy, he had been branded a traitor to his king and kin.

And it was there, in that haunted valley known as the Shrouded Vale, that they had met Fizzlewing—the strange, winged creature who'd led them through illusion and shadow, swooping to her rescue just as Drakor was about to finish her.

The wind stirred, carrying with it the scent of smoke and iron. All around lay the fallen—and those left to tend to them. Drelves wept over their dead; wings folded in mourning. The cries of the wounded cut through the stillness like ghosts that refused to fade. The elves grieved too; ear-tips lowered, eyes hollow as their boots scraped over stone and ash.

Lyria pressed a hand to her chest, feeling the throb of the mark beneath her palm—a reminder of what had been lost, and what still bound them all.

Then her gaze found Finnian, standing beside Eldrin. Ever loyal, twin blades strapped to his sides. He had secretly followed them out of the elven kingdom, risking his life to fight off the nemods that pursued them. Quick of hand, quicker of tongue; he had stood alone against the shadow panthers in the Dragon Graveyard—blinded by grief when he thought Eldrin and Lyria were lost forever. He fought the darkness alone until the light itself answered.

Her eyes lingered on Finnian a moment longer before looking at Eldrin again.

She looked down at her hand, her talons curling into her palms, remembering the feel of his fingers closing around hers in the fire and ruin—the silent promise neither of them had dared to speak aloud.

Was it gratitude that bound them? Or something far more dangerous?
The mark pulsed once beneath her skin, burning with an ache she couldn't name.

Whatever it was between them—whatever fate had tied their hands together—it was far from simple.

And as dawn broke over the smoldering hills, Lyria knew their fragile peace would not last.

Chapter 2

The smoke still lingered—low and clinging, as if the earth itself hadn't yet decided whether the battle was truly over.

From the broken wall of the drelf stronghold, Nyxari stood motionless, her padded feet pressed to the stone, her gaze cast over the quiet wreckage below. The battlefield still steamed where fire had singed the ground. Smoke hung low, drifting like ghosts across the fallen.

Beside her, Kaelis Skythorn said nothing.

They had stood like this before—years ago, after the razing of the Hollow. But this silence felt heavier. Charged.

Nyxari's eyes swept over the field, pausing on the familiar figure standing in the ash. Her wings—once blood-red—had changed. Now they shimmered silver-white, catching the thin rays of sunlight that broke through the smoke, as if the sky itself kissed her in reverence.

Lyria Ironwing.

And next to her… the Elven warrior.

His hand brushed Lyria's. Brief. Gentle. Unspoken.

Kaelis shifted.

Nyxari said nothing, but felt the younger drelf tense beside her like a bowstring drawn too far.

"She trusts him," Nyxari murmured.

"She shouldn't," Kaelis growled.

Her ears flattened. A hiss slipped through her teeth.

Nyxari glanced at her, the lines of memory pulling faint at her face. "You remember the day I found you both, don't you? Smoke on your skin. Ash in your lungs. Clutching each other like the world would split apart if you let go."

Kaelis didn't respond. Her eyes never left the pair below.

"You've guarded her ever since," Nyxari continued softly. "Even from herself."

"She doesn't see the danger," Kaelis whispered. "But I do."

The two drelves stood still on the wall, their shared history unspoken but present in every breath. War had orphaned Kaelis and Lyria, raised under Nyxari's watch—bonded not by blood, but by survival. Years of loss tempered their connection, forged in shadow and fire, holding fast like stone beneath a mountain.

Nyxari turned back toward the field. "He may be more than he seems."

"That's what I'm afraid of."

Without another word, Kaelis sprang from the wall.

Wings flared in a burst of purple and gold as she launched into the charred wind, climbing fast before banking hard—cutting straight toward the field. Toward Lyria.

Nyxari didn't stop her.

She only watched.

She had let go of them both long ago, knowing some paths must unfold beyond the reach of even the Veilkeeper.

Kaelis always moved with purpose. But today, the purpose burned sharper. Protective. Possessive. Afraid.

Nyxari's gaze shifted to Lyria, standing too close to the Elven warrior with the storm in his soul.

The Seer exhaled, ancient breath clouding the air.

They had once been inseparable — Kaelis and Lyria. Orphans of fire and sorrow. Raised together beneath her watchful eyes and the fractured sky of a realm that had forgotten its place in the world. Kaelis had always been the blade—sharp, swift, unbending. And Lyria, the fire beneath the stone. Different yet bound like roots beneath the mountain.

So, when Kaelis flew like that… Nyxari knew what would follow.

Not hatred. Not jealousy.

Fear.

Change was coming for them. For all of them.

And somewhere beneath the surface of it all, something else stirred.

Something no one has yet seen.

Kaelis landed hard, feet kicking up soot as her wings folded tight against her back. Her claws curled slightly with restraint.

Lyria turned at the sound—shoulders stiffening, eyes widening.

"Kaelis," she breathed, as if unsure whether to brace or embrace.

"Lyria." Her voice was flat. Too calm.

Eldrin stepped back instinctively, sensing the change in the air, the tightness in the stranger's stance.

Kaelis didn't look at him. Not yet. She kept her gaze on Lyria; her soot-marked cheeks and expression were unreadable. A softness Kaelis didn't like. Didn't trust.

She forced herself to glance at the elf warrior, meeting his eyes just long enough to make him shift uncomfortably. Then she looked back at Lyria.

"Who's this?" Kaelis said, nodding toward Eldrin.

"This is Eldrin. He saved my life," Lyria said slowly.

Kaelis's jaw tightened.

"We need to talk," she said.

Lyria hesitated. "Now?"

Kaelis leaned in, voice low. "Before I say something you'll regret hearing in front of him."

That did the trick.

Lyria nodded and took a step toward her.

Finnian, ever one to spot the spark before the fire, stepped in from the side and cleared his throat.

"Well now, I don't believe we've met," he said, offering a crooked grin and a slight bow. "Finnian of the Silver Rise". Twin-blade fighter, friend to prophecy-riddled warriors, and quite possibly the best-looking elf you'll meet today."

Kaelis stared at him.

Finnian blinked briefly, unsettled, then recovered. "No good?"

She finally turned her eyes fully onto him. "Speak again, and I'll turn those blades into earrings."

Finnian held up both hands. "Charmed," he muttered, already stepping aside.

Kaelis returned her gaze to Lyria. "Walk with me."

No room for arguments. No explanation.

Lyria followed.

They walked in silence, the battle-scarred ground crunching beneath their feet. The wind tugged faintly at their wings, carrying the faint scent of ash and blackened earth.

Kaelis didn't speak until they were well out of earshot—behind a shattered wall half-swallowed by ivy and shadow.

She turned to Lyria abruptly.

"What was that all about?" Kaelis demanded.

Lyria blinked. "What?"

"That..." Kaelis jerked her head back toward the battlefield. "I saw it from the wall. The way you touched him."

Lyria's jaw tightened, and a faint flush rose to her cheeks. "It was just… I don't know."

"He's an elf, Lyria."

"He saved my life. He helped us fight…"

"He's our en-e-my," Kaelis growled, drawing out each syllable like poison.

Silence stretched between them.

Kaelis folded her arms, her tail flicking once behind her in warning.

Lyria looked away. "You don't understand."

"I understand more than you think," Kaelis said, her voice low, steady. "I understand you bear a mark. Chosen for something ancient—something deadly. And now you're going to anchor yourself to an elf?"

Lyria turned sharply. "I'm not anchored to anyone," she snapped.

"Really?" Kaelis asked, eyes narrowing. "Are you sure about that?"

She took a step forward. "You've always led with your heart. It's one of the best things about you. But it's also how you get burned."

Lyria held her ground. "I'm not a hatchling anymore."

"No," Kaelis said. "But you're still the same Lyria who used to sneak out of the cavern just to find a patch of sky to dream under. And I'm still the one who dragged you back before the shadows found you."

They stared at each other—sisters of shadow and fire, still standing, still breathing, still stubborn.

Finally, Kaelis looked away, jaw tight.

"I'm not here to fight you," she said. "I just... I don't want to lose you to something we can't come back from."

Lyria's voice softened. "You won't lose me."

"You say that" Kaelis murmured, "but the world is already trying to change you. I see it. I feel it. And I don't know if I can stop it this time."

"You don't have to stop anything," Lyria said. "Because there's nothing to stop. That was just... a moment. That's all."

"A moment?" Kaelis's scowl deepened. "Can you hear yourself, Lyria?"

Anger surged within Lyria at the challenge—sharp and sudden. *How dare she question me?*

"Who do you think you are, anyway?" Lyria hissed, stepping forward and driving Kaelis back with the weight of her body. "My keeper?"

"No," Kaelis said, shaking her purple braids, holding her ground even as her claws scraped against the ash. "But I am here to remind you who you are—and what we stand for."

Before Lyria could answer, a sharp cry rose from the battlefield.

Both turned.

Around them, drelves and elves moved among the wounded—some carrying stretchers fashioned from cloaks and spears; others crouched beside fallen kin, whispering names like prayers. The battle had ended, but the grieving had only just begun.

One elf—young, bloodied, limping—stumbled as he tried to lift a wounded drelf twice his size. A second drelf dropped to help him without hesitation.

Lyria exhaled; her anger caught in her throat.

Kaelis said nothing. Her ears flicked back once, and her gaze drifted from the field to the horizon, where smoke still curled faintly against the sky.

The silence between them now felt different. Not resolved. But paused—like something waiting for breath.

Chapter 3

Eldrin watched Lyria and Kaelis from a distance; arms crossed, brow furrowed. He wasn't sure what Kaelis was to Lyria—but they were close. Close enough to argue.

He couldn't hear their words, but he didn't need to. The posture said enough—Lyria's stance was rigid; Kaelis's wings pinned tight against her spine. Both radiated heat in different ways.

And he knew why.

It was because of him.

An elf.

Watching them, Eldrin felt a strange twist in his chest. Even he didn't know what he and Lyria were to each other—how could anyone else? It was a bond he couldn't name, and one he didn't dare try to.

"Let me guess," Finnian murmured beside him. "That's the 'good to see you again' kind of talk?"

Eldrin didn't answer. Just glanced at his friend, who was watching the exchange with the same cautious curiosity—

though Finnian's gaze lingered a moment longer on Kaelis, brow raised.

"You think I should've kept my mouth shut?" Finnian asked.

Eldrin's lips twitched. "You? Quiet? That'll be the day."

Finnian crossed his arms, but his gaze drifted back to Kaelis, intrigued. There was a sharpness to her, all fire and fury, like she might scorch anyone who got too close—and yet, he couldn't look away.

Finnian let out a whistle. "That is one fiery drelf."

"They both are," Eldrin said, gaze fixed on the two drelves.

They exchanged a look—part amusement, part caution—as if both silently agreed not to get between the two drelves anytime soon.

Eldrin let out a slow breath as he noticed Lyria and the other drelf approaching. The air between them still crackled—sharp, electric, unfinished. It was in their brisk stride, the taut set of their shoulders, the agitated swish of their tails.

He knew that tension. Had worn it like armor. And he wasn't eager to have that fire aimed his way.

It would be hard for anyone to understand what the three of them had just survived.

Him… pulling Lyria from the edge of death in the Elven Forest.

The visions in the Shrouded Vale—visions that had rattled even Finnian's unshakable grin.

And the shadow panthers, claws like nightfall. Finnian fighting, bloodied but unyielding. How, Lyria leapt to save him when he fell.

Blood and fear etched the line between elves and drelves.

That wouldn't vanish overnight.

And truth be told, he wasn't sure how to handle any of it.

Where did they go from here?

The faint sound of wood on earth pulled Eldrin from his thoughts. It signaled Gantar's approach, leaning on his makeshift staff with one hand as he stepped up beside them. His gaze followed the same line as theirs—toward the two drelves now moving their way; tension still thrumming between them like an echo.

"Seems the storm is still brewing," Gantar said quietly.

Eldrin glanced at him. "They'll be all right… won't they?"

Gantar didn't answer right away. He studied Kaelis and Lyria, then nodded once—slow, unreadable.

"You two worked it out," Gantar said, looking from Eldrin to Finnian. "I suspect they will, too. Iron sharpens iron."

Eldrin didn't reply. He only met Finnian's gaze—and in that quiet glance, something unspoken passed between them. A shared memory of everything they'd already survived. A quiet acknowledgment that Gantar was, as usual, right.

A hush settled over the group as Lyria and Kaelis reached them. Neither spoke. The tension between them still clung to the air like smoke, but they stood side by side now—close enough to suggest the fire hadn't consumed them just yet.

A dry voice cut through the quiet.

"Well. Isn't this cozy?"

Thalendir stepped over a fallen nemod, his golden hair swept back in practiced disarray, armor singed at the shoulder. His hazel eyes flicked from Lyria to Kaelis, then settled on Eldrin with a crooked smirk.

"Still sparking chaos wherever you go, little brother?"

Eldrin crossed his arms. "Me? I'm a beacon of order."

Finnian snorted. "You'd think surviving shadow panthers might earn a touch more admiration."

Thalendir arched a brow. "You'd think."

But his gaze lingered on Eldrin for a heartbeat longer—just long enough to reveal something beneath the sarcasm.

Relief.

Or something dangerously close to it.

A deeper voice followed behind him. "We do not have the luxury of brotherly taunts."

King Eldermyst approached with a quiet authority that stilled the surrounding air. His silver-streaked hair caught the light, eyes sharp despite the wear of battle.

He surveyed the group—their soot-marked faces, torn tunics, and silent stares.

His gaze paused briefly on Lyria. Then, Kaelis. Then, Gantar.

"There is much to be done," he said. "The wounded must be tended. The dead honored. And this realm—" he turned toward the broken gates of the drelf stronghold, "—will not rebuild itself."

His voice carried no judgment. Only weight. Duty.

"Forgive me. I am King Eldermyst, ruler of the Elven realm… and father to Eldrin."

A nod toward his younger son.

"And this," he added with a faint smile, "is Thalendir—my eldest. And, depending on the day, as you can tell, my most endearing."

Lyria stepped forward, shoulders squared despite the exhaustion in her limbs. Ash clung to her wings, still folded tight.

"I am Lyria Ironwing," she said, voice steady. "Daughter of the Drelf Realm". And this," she motioned to her side, "is Kaelis Skythorn, my kin in all but blood."

Kaelis gave a curt nod, her sky-blue eyes flicking briefly to Eldermyst and Thalendir without bowing. Not defiant—but not deferent either.

King Eldermyst inclined his head in return, studying them both with the quiet intensity of a ruler who missed nothing.

"Your courage today will not be forgotten," he said simply.

"And your aid to our kingdom will be remembered long after this smoke has faded," Lyria said, offering a slight bow.

"Speaking of your kingdom…" the king echoed, his voice unreadable, lingering just long enough on the phrase to draw a line she couldn't ignore.

Lyria's spine straightened. "Not your concern. You and your warriors have done enough."

The words landed harsher than she had intended, but she didn't take them back.

Eldermyst's gaze narrowed slightly. "Did your king survive the battle?"

Lyria replied coolly, "The drelves have no king. We do not place the fate of an entire realm into the hands of one voice." She let her eyes flick to Eldrin before returning to the king.

"We have a council. Or we did—before the attack shattered half of them. But we will rebuild. Together."

"I see…" the king murmured, his eyes narrowing ever so slightly in thought.

Gantar stepped forward; his voice measured. "We'll help—if you'll have us."

Then, with a respectful glance toward the king. "That is… if it's acceptable to you, my liege."

King Eldermyst gave a solemn nod. "Of course, we must help. I will leave some of my warriors behind, but I need to return to the Elven kingdom before nightfall. We need to secure the border. And Orendir, along with my fallen warriors, deserves to be laid to rest beneath the sky they protected."

Silence followed.

Lyria exhaled softly, her gaze drifting over the wreckage. Rebuilding the walls, honoring the dead, comforting the grieving… it would all take time. Help would be welcome, regardless of her preference.

"You should rest awhile," she said at last. "Let us tend to your wounded before you depart. It's the least we can offer."

"We will regroup, but not for long," said the king.

No one argued.

Around them, the smoke thinned, and the wind shifted—but the weight of what remained would take far longer to clear.

Then—

A blur of wings spun into view, glitter trailing behind it like stardust.

Fizzlewing.

He twirled lazily through the air, upside-down at first, before flipping upright with an exaggerated flourish and landing—light as a leaf—on Gantar's shoulder.

"Whew," he said, brushing nonexistent dust from his tunic. "I leave you alone for one war and look what you've done to the place."

Finnian groaned. "You again?"

"I can tell you're happy to see me," Fizzlewing said brightly.

Eldrin straightened. "You said there was another mark?"

Fizzlewing's smile didn't fade, but it sharpened. "I did."

"Where?" Finnian asked. "Who?"

The pixie fluttered into the air and crossed his legs mid-hover, wings beating lazily. "That's the tricky part. I felt it stir—like a ripple in the weave—but where it landed?" He shrugged. "Not even I could say."

Eldrin exchanged a look with Gantar, who had gone still suddenly.

"And if the darkness finds it first?" Eldrin asked.

Fizzlewing's tone dropped.

"Then the war you just survived… will feel like a whisper."

Chapter 4

Zyressa stood at the edge of a jagged cliff. The winds howled like spirits torn from the deep. Far below, the scorched valley of ash stretched like a wound across the land, the remains of Korrath's domain smoldering in ruin.

She had felt it.

Not the mark. But something just as dangerous.

A shift in power.

Her emerald eyes narrowed as she gazed toward the volcanic spires beyond. Vartharax vanished from the skies—retreating to the old fortress of black stone and flame. Drakor had not returned to him.

Good.

A vacuum where chaos would grow. One that might clear the way for her.

She curled her talons against the stone, her scarred scales catching the light of a low blood moon. She had watched from the shadows for too long. Now, Korrath was gone. Drakor disgraced. The time of silence is over.

A flicker of movement caught her eye. A shadow coasted along the ridge.

She didn't flinch as another dragon landed beside her—lighter, leaner, with silver-blue eyes that held secrets like knives. Not a dragon she trusted. But one she remembered.

"Zyressa," the rogue said, voice low against the wind.

She didn't turn. "Didn't expect to see you crawling out of the ashes."

The rogue snorted. "I might say the same."

The air between them thinned. Then—

"The world is shifting," the rogue continued. "And if you want to survive what comes next… you'll listen."

Zyressa's tail lashed once behind her.

"I'm listening."

"The mark's awakening is weakening Vartharax. He's lost both his commanders…"

Zyressa's wings twitched. "Everyone knows the drelves claimed the mark."

The rogue's gaze darkened. "I'm not speaking of the first."

Zyressa turned to face him, the wind curling through her green crests. "There's another?"

The rogue nodded. "It stirs. And the dark clves feel it too."

Zyressa narrowed her eyes. "The dark elves?"

"They grow restless," the rogue said grimly. "And not just whispers. Old pacts are reawakening—ones that even Vartharax doesn't control."

Zyressa let that settle.

Then she smiled. Slow. Calculated.

"Good."

The rogue dragon tilted his head, watching her smile with wary calculation.

"You could take their place," he said at last, his voice just above the wind. "Vartharax won't trust Drakor again. And Korrath's corpse still smolders in the ash."

Zyressa's wings unfurled partway, the membrane catching the moonlight like green fire. "And you think I should go groveling for the dark lord's favor?"

"Not grovel," the rogue replied. "Position."

She huffed, amused. "There's little difference."

"But there's opportunity," he said. "The dark elves want the mark as badly as Vartharax does. Perhaps more. They've begun moving in secret. Reaching out."

Zyressa narrowed her eyes. "To you?"

"To those like me. Outcasts. Observers. One's not blinded by old loyalties."

He stepped closer, talons scraping the stone. "If you reach them first—align yourself with their cause—you won't need to serve Vartharax. You'll have something he wants. And power enough to make him kneel."

Zyressa considered that in silence.

The idea coiled inside her like a promise. She had no interest in serving. But commanding? That was different.

"You expect me to trust shade-walkers and exiles?" She said coolly.

"I'm offering you a chance to rise while the others fall," the rogue countered. "The drelf mark was the first. But the second—wherever it lands—will change everything. If we find it before the others…"

Zyressa's gaze turned toward the dark horizon. A low rumble echoed across the volcanic ridge.

"If the dark elves truly move again," she said slowly, "then the old pacts are stirring."

"They are. And they remember you, Zyressa. They will follow if you lead."

She turned her head slightly, one brow raised. "Is that meant to flatter or warn?"

The rogue dragon smiled. "Both."

Zyressa flexed her claws, mind already weaving the next move. She would not grovel. She would not kneel. But she would play their game—so long as she could win it.

"Then take me to them," she said.

The rogue dipped his head once, wings spreading in a sweep of shadow. Wind rose fierce and cold, carrying the promise of storms.

Zyressa leapt from the cliff with a thunderous beat of her wings; her emerald form vanishing into the shadows—chasing power, chasing prophecy, chasing the second mark.

Somewhere in the shadowed lands beyond the volcanic ridge, old fires were being stoked again—but not all of them would wait for Zyressa to arrive.

The wind carried the scent of fear. A wounded creature staggered through the thorns, scales torn and breathing ragged. It had once served the dragons—long ago. Now it was something lesser, crawling across the burnt ground, trying to escape whatever hunted the night. The surrounding shadows pulsed, silent but alive. It glanced back. Nothing.

Then— A rush of air. A claw struck from above, slamming the creature to the ground with brutal force. Ash scattered in every direction.

The creature whimpered. “Mercy…”

Above it loomed something hunched and crooked, wings torn, yellow eyes burning like dying coals. He leaned close, nostrils flaring, his voice a rasp edged with heat.

"Mercy?" The voice was a rasp of smoke and fire. "You think mercy kept me alive while Korrath burned?"

The creature trembled. "They said you were gone… devoured by the dark."

A grin cut across the dragon's muzzle—crooked, cruel.

"I'm alive," he rasped as his wings twitched. "And hungry."

Flame erupted from his jaws. The creature's scream vanished into the roar.

When silence returned, only drifting ash marked the grave.

From the tree line beyond, something else moved—a presence vast and voiceless; its gaze cold as the void. Watching. Waiting. Whispering.

Drakor turned toward it, the firelight painting his scales in shades of green and ruin. With a single, shuddering beat of his wings, he rose into the night—the forest bowing beneath the gust—until only the echo of his flight remained.

Chapter 5

On the battlefield below the drelf ramparts, warriors moved among the fallen. Some loaded the dead onto carts. Others tended the wounded; their voices hushed. Gantar walked among them, his hands steady, his gaze heavy with grief.

King Eldermyst led his horse through the mayhem, his boots crunching over trampled earth and shards of stone. Both his sons walked at his side, smoke from the dying fires curling around them.

"You'll remain here," the king said to Eldrin, voice low and firm. "Help them rebuild. Show them that not all elves are bound by the old hatred."

Eldrin nodded, though the weight of the battlefield pressed heavily on his shoulders. "And the prophecy? You heard Fizzlewing. He said there is another mark. I need to understand what it means—what my part in it is."

The king's eyes lingered on him. "You trust that little creature?"

"Yes, Father. He's… a character. But he's on our side."

A faint smile tugged at the king's mouth. "Then seek the truth. But tread carefully. The darkness hasn't retreated—it's only searching for someone new to devour."

He turned to Thalendir. "You'll stay as well."

Thalendir stiffened. "But Father—"

"No arguing," the king said, his tone sharp enough to cut the words from his son's mouth. "This will be a lesson you need. As future king, you'll require more than tactics and titles. Let this place remind you what war truly is."

Thalendir's jaw flexed as his gaze swept the broken ramparts and the mingling of elves and drelves. To remain here—to labor beside them—felt like an insult he could barely endure. But one glance at his father's unyielding expression silenced him. He exhaled through his nose and gave a shallow bow, obedience without surrender.

"They may not have marble halls," the king added coolly, "but they fought with more courage than most I've known."

"I suppose I'll make the most of it, Father," Thalendir said, his voice smooth, but each word carried a sharpened edge. "If shoveling rubble with drelves is what you desire." His hair caught the wind like a frayed banner as he folded his arms across his chest.

King Eldermyst's brows drew together, his glare cutting through the brisk air. "I desire the future king to learn humility."

Thalendir smirked. "Of course, Father. I'll… reflect on that. Nothing like mud and smoke to teach a prince his place."

The king said no more. He watched as they lifted a wounded drelf onto a cart in the courtyard below, as the drelf cried out. Gantar bent over him, staff in hand, murmuring old words of comfort. A soft golden glow flickered under the sage's fingers. When the soldier's pain eased, the sage exhaled and rose, leaning on his staff.

Eldermyst descended a path strewn with debris toward him. For a moment, the old healer did not look up, lost in the work of easing suffering. When he finally met the king's gaze, the air between them thickened with unspoken things.

"I owe you an apology," the king said. "For doubting you. For… allowing them to chain you like a traitor."

Gantar tilted his head, a wisp of dry humor in his eyes. "And here I thought kings didn't apologize."

"I don't," Eldermyst replied, the corner of his mouth twitching. "But for you, I'll make an exception."

Gantar let out a breath, not quite a laugh, not quite forgiveness. "It's not me, you betrayed. It's what Thariel believed in."

The king's expression faltered at her name. "I intend to make it right. I can't change the past, but I can ask for your help in mending what's broken."

Gantar's gaze softened. "You're leaving, then?"

"Yes. The elves need their king. There are burials to complete… and a Council to face."

"Orendir," Gantar said softly.

"He died protecting what we swore to preserve," the king said, his voice roughening. "He will not be forgotten. I want you with me to set things right. With the Council. With the kingdom. With her memory."

Gantar's hand brushed the Aetherstone at his neck, the weight of old vows stirring. After a long silence, he nodded. "I'll return with you. But I'm not done with the prophecy."

"Nor am I," said the king. "That's why Eldrin remains. He will follow where it leads."

The decision settled between them like the closing of a door as the wind carried the faint toll of distant bells — a kingdom breathing again, if only for a moment.

Before departing, Gantar sought Eldrin and Lyria, beckoning them to a quiet stretch of wall where the wind whispered through shattered stone. They followed without a word.

"The days ahead will test more than your strength," he said, facing them. "They will test your heart. The mark and the dagger have bound your paths together, whether the realms accept it or not." His gaze lingered on Lyria, then Eldrin. "Trust one another, even when doubt whispers louder than reason."

Lyria's wings twitched. "Kaelis… she thinks this path is dangerous. That I'm forgetting who I am."

"And perhaps she is right," Gantar said gently. "To bridge a divide, one must step onto both shores. But remember—bridges are built to be crossed, not burned."

Eldrin swallowed and nodded. "I won't fail her. Or you."

The old sage smiled faintly. "It isn't failure that destroys us, Eldrin. It's pride."

He reached up and touched the pendant at his neck—a pale shard flecked with faint blue light.

"This," he said, "was once part of the Aetherstone. I carved it long ago for your mother. She left it to me when she passed. To keep it safe… until such a time as this."

Eldrin glanced down at his own pendant—the larger, glowing Aetherstone that now pulsed softly at his side.

"So, the stone connects us?" He asked quietly.

"When the world falls silent, listen to it," Gantar said. "The stone will guide you. And if you wear it, we are not truly apart."

A thin ribbon of pale light stitched itself along the rampart and settled on the torch bracket with a soft hiss.

"Fizzlewing," Eldrin breathed.

The little sprite tilted in the light, wings whispering. "Stone makes my wings itch," he said, nose wrinkling at the black rock and iron pins. "The ward-stones here hum. They don't like my kind."

"You're leaving?" Eldrin asked, trying not to sound disturbed.

"For a little while," Fizzlewing chimed. "The second light is stirring, and the Vale hears things long halls do not. I'll follow the thread where torches can't." His bright eyes flicked to the pouch at Eldrin's side. "Listen, when the world goes quiet."

"Thank you for saving my life," Lyria said, fingering the stone flower in her hand. "Will you come if we need you?" She asked, swallowing hard.

Fizzlewing hovered closer, voice going small and solemn. "If you call loud enough, Silver Wings, I'll hear."

He touched Lyria's wing with a fleeting spark; his face flushed.

Eldrin's mouth tightened. "Any hint where the next mark will fall?"

"Closer than you think," Fizzlewing whispered, with a smile like a secret.

He tapped his tail; a single spark jumped, then went dark.

"Keep your head down and your sword sharp. And remember…"

His tone softened, almost fond.

"The deeper the dark, the brighter the light must burn."

Then he was gone—up and out over the ramparts, a flick of pale light drawn thin against the sky—leaving only the faint smell of rain and the feeling that the air itself had been listening.

When the spark died, silence closed over the wall. They watched the shadows where he had hovered; none dared to break the stillness. Lyria's wings dipped, as though she felt the absence most keenly.

It was Finnian who finally muttered, "Strange how a little thing can leave so large a space behind."

Eldrin and Lyria turned. Finnian had quietly joined them; his cloak pulled tight, his usual grin tempered by something softer.

"Never thought I'd hear you say that" Lyria said, studying him.

Finnian shrugged, a faint smile lighting his eyes. "Even mischief has its moments."

A voice called from below—the king was ready to depart.

Gantar rested a hand on each of their shoulders, the weight of it both grounding and reluctant. He exhaled, a sigh that carried more than fatigue—sorrow, pride, and something like hope.

Then he turned toward the wagons, cloak brushing the stone as he went.

Thalendir crossed his path, scowling. The two regarded one another for a long, silent moment.

"Mind your brother," Gantar said at last. "A leader is measured by the lives he lifts, not the shadows he casts. Your mother would be proud of how you came to your brothers' aid."

Thalendir's jaw tightened. "Your praise is generous, old sage—but don't mistake duty for affection." His eyes flicked briefly to Eldrin before he turned and stalked away.

Gantar watched the prince go, his expression unreadable. As he approached Duskrunner and swung into the saddle, he glanced once more toward the retreating prince.

You hide it well, Thalendir; he thought. *But I saw it on the road—the part of you that still remembers how to care.*

The wagons creaked into motion, bearing the wounded and the shrouded dead. Hooves and wheels echoed through the courtyard as the company filed out, King Eldermyst at their head, his silver-clad stallion gleaming even in the gloom.

Eldrin watched them disappear into the trees, swallowed by mist and distance. Beside him, Lyria's tail waved behind her. Kaelis stood rigid, her wings flicking in silent thought.

Finnian broke the hush. "There they go. Back to their towers and banners… and here we are, stuck with the mess."

Eldrin exhaled slowly. "We'll make something of it."

Finnian smirked faintly. “Better make it fast. I already miss hot bread and clean clothes.”

They stood in silence as the last echoes of the king’s company faded. The courtyard felt suddenly larger; the wind colder, and the weight of what lay ahead pressed down on them like the shadow of the mountains.

Chapter 6

They moved like shadows beneath the canopy, cloaked in silence. The Arden stretched around them—vast, ancient, and breathing with secrets. Strange mushrooms with pumpkin-orange heads pushed through the rot, pulsing faintly as if drawing breath. Low brambles curled like sleeping serpents; their thorns hidden beneath veils of leaf and vine.

No outsider had walked these depths in centuries. The forest did not welcome strangers—but it remembered these drifters.

Flames flickered low in a ring of blackened stone, casting jagged shapes across the cloaked figures. Hoods hid their faces—and the sharp points of their ears—but not the glint of their eyes: onyx, reflecting firelight like polished obsidian. None spoke. Not yet.

At last, a voice broke the silence—smooth and patient as a serpent's breath.

"It stirs."

A murmur rippled through the circle like wind through dead leaves.

"The second mark has awakened," the voice continued. "And with it, the balance shifts again. Each mark tips the scales of the realms—light or dark, peace or ruin. The first fell to the drelf. The next must be ours."

From the shadows came a low, dry laugh. "The realms forget," whispered the voice, colder now, "that darkness remembers its prophecies too."

The fire cracked.

Beyond the ring, something shifted in the trees. The old forest knew the tread of unnatural things—and made no sound to warn against it.

"Do we know where the second mark will appear?" asked a female elf, her voice smooth but edged like a blade.

The serpent-voiced speaker tilted their head. "There are signs… but not yet certainty. Only whispers."

A darker shadow lingered just beyond the circle, silent, unseen. Not an ally. Not an enemy. Watching. Waiting.

The dark elves—known among their kind as the Umbrin—moved like smoke through the Arden. They did not know he was there. Not yet.

The speaker raised a hand toward the fire. "The balance tilts toward the light. Korrath is dead. Drakor disgraced.

Vartharax retreats. And in the north…" A pause, a hiss of breath. "A drelf with silver wings walks among elves."

A murmur rippled through the group—anger, disbelief.

"She bears the first mark," the speaker said. "If we do not claim the second, the scales will tip beyond recall. And when light reigns unchallenged."

They leaned forward, eyes glinting in the dark. "Darkness dies."

The fire guttered low, then flared again—burning black at its heart.

From the woods, the unseen watcher seethed. Smoke coiled from his nostrils, curling through the night like a warning.

They spoke his name like a curse.

Like he was nothing.

He could have burst from the shadows then—fire on his tongue, wings tearing the canopy apart—but he did not.

Patience was a weapon. One he had learned too well.

A new voice rose from the Umbrin circle—low, weighted with age and veiled power. "We waited long enough. The mark is near. We must be ready."

"And if we can't find it?" the female elf asked, her tone sharp as drawn steel.

Silence answered her. Only the hiss of fire and the whisper of wings.

Branches shifted overhead. Leaves spiraled down like falling embers.

Then—a shadow broke from the treetops, descending in a rush of wind and scale.

Talons struck the soil, punching deep. Firelight shimmered across green armor.

Zyressa.

She landed at the edge of the fire's reach, voice a low rasp that carried like smoke. "Then you will have help. The forest is not the only place darkness remembers."

A murmur ran through the circle—uneasy, intrigued.

"Zyressa…" The serpent-tongued Drovane inclined his hooded head, his tone threading between reverence and caution. "We are… pleased to have you. I wasn't certain you would answer."

The dragon's emerald eyes glinted in the firelight. "I heard your call," she said. "Whispers through the forest. Rumors carried on the wind." Her tail scraped the earth. "But tell me—what is it you offer?"

Drovane shifted. "Power. A place among us. A share in the mark's awakening."

"A share?" Her teeth gleamed. "You called me for scraps?"

The murmurs sharpened, echoing through the blackened trees.

Then the branches shivered again, and another shape dropped from above—silver-blue scales flashing.

Velthar, the rogue dragon.

"She is here because I called her," he said, tail carving a slow line in the soil. His eyes fixed on Zyressa with the slow, deliberate weight of a hunter choosing his strike. "What we offer depends on what you know."

Zyressa's wings twitched, but she did not flinch.

Velthar bared his teeth. "Speak carefully. These are not elves you can toy with. They have waited centuries for their moment—and they are not patient."

The Umbrin leaned closer, hunger burning in their eyes.

Zyressa let the silence stretch, weighing their desire against her own. Finally, her tail flicked, scattering embers toward the trees. "I did not come blind. After Korrath fell and Drakor fled, I searched the caverns they had abandoned. The stones remember whispers, and I found remnants they left behind."

The dark elves shifted. Even Velthar tilted his head.

She gave them only a taste: "The second light will awaken in the blood of the forest-born…"

A collective breath shivered through the circle.

"The elves…" hissed one of thc Umbrin.

"Yes," Zyressa's voice was soft, almost reverent. "I believe the elf who defied his own kind to save a drelf will bear the mark—or lead us to it."

A ripple of interest moved through the gathering.

"And… we have a lure he cannot resist," Drovane continued, lifting his hooded head toward the firelight. "One born of both flame and shadow—beautiful beyond belief. Her soul is Umbrin. Her heart, draconic. The perfect bridge between their world and ours."

A tremor rippled along Zyressa's wings—subtle but unmistakable. Her slit pupils widened, catching the fire's reflection like molten emerald.

"Oh…" she breathed, a low, dangerous purr curling beneath her words. "How exquisite."

The air tightened. Even the Umbrin shadows stilled.

A murmur spread through the circle. Someone whispered a name.

Camyra.

"She waits beyond the veil," Drovane said, the corners of his mouth curving in satisfaction. "Bound by darkness, patient as hunger itself. When the time comes, she will set her claws deep into his heart. All we must do is draw him out."

He leaned forward, voice lowering to a whisper that slid through the smoke like a serpent through ash.

"She will do the rest."

Velthar's tail lashed once. "And how, my dark friends, do you plan to lure him without alerting the others?"

Dark smiles flickered in the firelight, but Drovane offered nothing more.

The fire hissed. Sparks spiraled into the black canopy.

A presence lingered.

No one saw the figure crouched deeper in the dark. Wings torn. Eyes smoldering.

Drakor.

If they found the second mark first… they would claim it.

No.

He would not allow that.

The dark had always been his ally. And in that darkness, he saw the truth: he knew more than Zyressa, more than the Umbrin. He had studied the prophecy, traced the runes. He alone could read the signs.

A curl of smoke slipped from his jaws as his thoughts drifted to his last kill—small, swift, brittle in the bones. A skitterling.

There had been one… There would be others. The small things could creep into places larger hunters could not.

The corner of his mouth curled.

Perhaps not all the old creatures had outlived their usefulness.

He moved into the clearing, shadow swallowing shadow. His presence stretched long across the fire, drawing every gaze until the circle's hunger shifted to him.

A ripple of unease moved through the circle. Some shifted back, wary of crooked wings and the raw violence that hummed in the surrounding air. Others leaned forward, drawn to the hunger in his presence.

Drakor did not so much as glance at their reactions. He locked his gaze on Drovane, and he pressed into the fire-lit ring, making it feel smaller and tighter.

Zyressa's tail twitched once, a faint rasp against the earth, though her face betrayed nothing.

The flames popped, sending a spray of sparks skyward. Shadows jumped along the trees like startled prey.

When Drakor finally spoke, his voice was low, deliberate. "I can deliver the elf," he said.

No one moved. Only the fire hissed, and the Arden seemed to lean in to listen.

"You want him," Drakor said. Smoke curled from his nostrils. "I know how to make him come to you… and you won't even have to chase."

A hush passed through the circle—shoulders tensed beneath black cloaks, eyes narrowing to slits of light. The Umbrin did not rise or draw steel, yet the fire's glow caught on their hoods, gleaming like blades half-drawn in the dark.

Zyressa's tail stilled, the faintest twitch of her wings betraying that she had not expected him. Velthar's expression didn't shift, but his head angled—fractionally—as though weighing the advantage of letting Drakor speak versus tearing him apart where he stood.

Drovane alone stepped forward, the serpent's smile sliding back across his face. "Drakor…" he murmured, tasting the name. "We thought you… diminished."

"Not diminished," Drakor said, smoke coiling in lazy threads. "Re-focused."

No one moved. Even the fire seemed to hesitate, its hiss swallowed by the Arden's deeper silence. The circle had shifted—subtly, irreversibly—and every figure there knew it.

In the space between heartbeats, the hunt had changed hands.

Chapter 7

The sun set red over the broken battlements, catching on shards of frost that clung to the drelf stonework. Lyria's breath misted in the chill as she hauled another beam toward the wall. Around her, elves and drelves moved like two halves of a severed army—never quite touching, never quite trusting. Every clang of a hammer echoed the unspoken truth: this was a truce built on splintered bones, and one wrong word could crack it apart.

Eldrin appeared at her side, carrying a timber with effortless strength. His green eyes searched her face, but she kept her gaze on the wall.

"Let my warriors and I do the heavy lifting," he said. His tone was casual; a smile flicked across his face. "You just direct us."

"I don't need you to carry my load," she replied, sharper than intended. The words frosted in the cold air between them.

He hesitated, clearly wanting to say more, but Kaelis's voice carried across the courtyard, barking orders at a pair of elves who were dragging stone too close to the drelf supply stores.

Lyria stiffened. Kaelis's presence was a reminder of the argument that had burned like a scar between them.

You're forgetting who you are, Kaelis had hissed after the battle. *He's an elf, Lyria. Our enemy.*

Since then, Lyria had drawn her wings tighter, her walls higher. Kaelis was right. They are elves; we are drelves. And no matter what had transpired between them, nothing would ever change that.

Eldrin finally broke the silence. "If I offended you—"

"You didn't," she cut in quickly. "This isn't about you."

But of course, it was, and they both knew it.

A sharp clang split the air as a length of timber struck stone. Across the courtyard, Thalendir stood bristling beside a toppled beam, his golden hair catching the sun like a crown of fire. A young drelf crouched nearby, eyes wide, claws digging into the dirt.

"You could have crushed me," Thalendir snapped. "Do you even know how to handle that properly?"

The drelf's nostrils flared, wings twitching. "I was doing fine until you shoved me," he growled, his voice carrying.

Around them, work stopped. Hammers hung in mid--air. A few elves tightened their grips on their tools; a group of drelves bared teeth and hissed.

Kaelis was already moving, her braids swinging as she strode across the courtyard. "Step away from him, elf," she said, voice like a drawn blade. "You strike one of my kin again, and you'll regret it."

"Your kin dropped the timber," Thalendir retorted, his hand twitching near his sword. "I only saved us from losing another wall."

"Saved?" Kaelis's laugh was sharp and cold. "You'd rather see a Drelf crushed than lend a hand."

Lyria felt her stomach knot as she glanced at Eldrin. He was already moving, slipping between the two groups as the air crackled with the promise of violence.

"Stop it!" His voice rang across the courtyard, commanding but tight. "We're rebuilding a stronghold, not tearing it apart again." He leveled a warning look at Thalendir first, then Kaelis. "If either of you wants to fight, save it for the nemods and the shadow panthers—because if they return tonight, we'll need all the strength we can muster."

For a heartbeat, no one moved. Then Kaelis hissed something under her breath in the Drelf tongue and hauled the young warrior back toward the wall. Thalendir muttered a curse and stooped to lift the beam himself, his jaw tight.

Lyria's wings shifted restlessly, the tension in the courtyard seeping into her bones. This alliance was a rope fraying at both ends, and she could feel it straining with every heartbeat.

From the corner of the courtyard, Finnian caught her eye and gave a half-shrug, as if to say, *'This is only going to get worse.'* But his gaze slid past her toward the forest beyond the walls.

Something moved there. Just a flicker of pale light between the trees.

Finnian frowned, rubbing his eyes. When he looked again, the forest was still—silent, watching.

"Did anyone see that?" he asked.

Eldrin glanced over, eyebrows raised. "What"

"Hmm." Finnian stared a moment longer, then shook his head. "Could've sworn I saw — never mind."

By nightfall, the stronghold had quieted. Workers patched cracked stone with timber and mortar, reinforced makeshift barricades, and shored up the eastern rampart with fresh supports. Torches flared along the outer ledges, their flickering light casting long shadows across the cliff-side walls. Lookouts stood at attention in their wooden towers, eyes scanning the dark forests beyond.

But within the stone walls, life pulsed on.

Into the cliffside's inner stronghold, angular passageways and arched stone corridors formed like veins beneath the earth. Heavy shutters could secure the gathering halls against a siege on one side. Thick wooden beams framed the ceilings. Smoke drifted upward through narrow vents carved high into the rock.

Lyria invited the elves in, though few looked comfortable. They clustered near the entrance to the main hall, where the stone was warmer from the fire and the air less heavy. The walls curved in natural arcs, carved to follow the grain of the mountain rather than against it, their surfaces etched with spirals that caught the light like ripples on water.

Drelves moved through the space with quiet purpose — their steps unhurried, but never idle. Some carried heavy wooden trays bearing slabs of meat, seared only on the edges, the centers still deep red. Others passed stone bowls of thin, spiced broth and platters of dark bread crisped over the hearth. No knives or forks were offered; the drelves tore the meat with claw-tipped fingers, dipping it into the broth before eating.

The smell was rich and smoky, undercut by a faint metallic tang that made Eldrin's mouth tighten. It was nothing like the game stews of the Elven Realm — this was primal, unvarnished, the kind of meal meant to fuel strength rather than please the eye.

Thalendir accepted his portion with the same poise he used for court banquets — but his eyes lingered a moment too long on the meat's crimson center. His jaw tightened almost imperceptibly before he took a deliberate bite, chewing as though to prove something.

Kaelis's gaze flicked toward him, catching the hesitation. One corner of her mouth curved — not quite a smile, more an acknowledgment that the proud prince was out of his element.

He swallowed, then muttered just loud enough for Eldrin to hear, "Barbarian fare. I suppose it suits the place."

Eldrin tore off a piece of bread, dipped it into the broth, and took a slow bite before replying in a voice just as low. "Strange… it seems to suit you."

Thalendir's eyes narrowed, but he didn't answer — only set his jaw and took another bite, this one sharper, as if to silence the remark.

Kaelis, still watching from across the table, gave Eldrin the faintest approving glance before looking away.

Finnian, meanwhile, caught that glance and decided to earn one of his own. He tore into the meat with exaggerated enthusiasm, even humming his approval. "Delicious," he announced, flashing Kaelis a grin.

Her gaze shifted to him, cool as winter stone. "You're chewing it wrong."

Finnian blinked. "There's a wrong way to chew?"

"Apparently," she said, and turned back to her own meal, leaving him staring after her with a lopsided grin that was part wounded pride, part challenge accepted.

Eldrin hid a smirk behind his cup, noting the look on his friend's face. He'd seen Finnian size up a thousand opponents in training — but never quite like this.

Across the table, Kaelis kept her expression neutral, though inwardly she fought a flicker of amusement. One wing gave the faintest twitch — a tell she quickly stilled — before she reached for another slice of bread. The elf was bold — reckless, even — and far too quick to think he could earn her favor with a grin and a compliment. Still, there was something disarming in the way he didn't seem to fear her. She pushed the thought aside, reminding herself she was only tolerating the elves for Lyria's sake.

Finnian, oblivious to her dismissal, leaned back with his cup in hand. "Well," he said under his breath, just loud enough for Eldrin to hear, "I think she likes me."

Eldrin didn't bother to hide his smirk this time. "I think you're mistaking that twitch, Finnian. That was a warning shot."

Finnian grinned. "Warnings mean they noticed you."

"Or they want to eat you," Eldrin replied.

"Details," Finnian said, and took another sip, entirely ignoring the sidelong glance from Kaelis that promised he'd learn better — the hard way.

Eldrin spotted Lyria near a storeroom arch, speaking with one of the drelf elders. Her voice was low, measured, steady in a way that belied the exhaustion etched into her stance.

She stood tall, her wings folded close, but he could see the weight she carried in the small details: the way her fingers tightened around each other, the faint slump of her shoulders when she thought no one was watching.

He lingered a moment, unseen in the bustle of the courtyard, watching her. She didn't look like the fugitive he'd first met in the forest, nor the wounded warrior from the Vale. She looked like a leader—wary, tempered by battle, but still burning with purpose.

When the elder inclined his head and moved away, Eldrin crossed the distance quietly.

"You've built something strong here," he said, lowering himself onto a stone bench nearby.

"We've had to," Lyria replied without looking at him.

A young drelf approached, whispered something in her ear, then darted away. Lyria's jaw tightened—barely—but Eldrin caught it.

He leaned forward. "What is it?"

She hesitated, then exhaled. "Our food stores have dwindled. The smoke masked it at first, but we've lost more than we thought."

He scanned the room. Elves and drelves alike sat huddled with their bowls, eating quietly, scraping every bit from the bottom. Grateful for warmth—but clearly still hungry.

"I'll take a hunting party out at first light," Eldrin offered.

"You don't have to," Lyria blurted.

"I know," he said, tone steady. "But I want to. It might help us earn favor among your drelves. Besides…" He glanced around. "Keeping us occupied elsewhere seems like a good idea."

Lyria's eyes narrowed as she studied him. "Then take Kaelis—and maybe a scout or two. These lands don't answer to Elven feet. There are dangers out there you know nothing about."

"I'll take whoever you recommend," he replied, a faint smile tugging at his lips. "Any help to keep us from getting lost—or skewered—is welcome."

She didn't return the smile, but her expression softened.

Then her voice dropped. "Do you think they'll come back?"

"Who?" Eldrin asked, suddenly alert.

She hesitated, wings shifting slightly. "The panthers. The nemods. Or whatever else the darkness sends. We wounded them… but we didn't destroy them."

Eldrin nodded slowly, his jaw tightening. "Our connection—our power—together it should hold the darkness at bay. For now, at least. But we need to find the next mark bearer. Any ideas?"

Lyria shook her head. "None." She hesitated, gaze flicking toward a shadowed corridor off the main hall. "But perhaps the white dragon will give me guidance."

"Any clues would help," Eldrin said. "I wish Gantar were here. He would know where to start."

Her eyes searched his face, noting the slump in his shoulders, the way the fire in him seemed to burn low. "We all need rest," she said, her voice softening. "I'll have someone show you to your quarters."

"Thanks, but I'll stay with my warriors. We can sleep here." He gestured to the stone floor.

Lyria stiffened. "Why do you insult us?"

"What?"

"Do you think we are so savage," she snapped, "that we wouldn't offer our guests' beds beneath a proper roof?"

"That's not what I meant—" Eldrin took a step back, as if struck.

"That's the problem with you elves." Her voice was quiet now, but it cut all the deeper. "You don't think."

And with a flick of her tail, she turned and walked away, leaving the firelight to dance over his stunned expression.

Eldrin exhaled slowly. He didn't understand her. She had risked her life for him—yet now she was cold, guarded, as though nothing had ever passed between them.

He stayed there for a while, leaning against a stone pillar, watching the firelight dance along the carved walls. The murmurs of the hall faded to a low hum — the soft clatter of armor, the faint scrape of quills as reports were written, the kind of quiet that follows victory but never quite feels like peace.

Eldrin exhaled slowly, the weight of the day settling heavily across his shoulders.

Across the room, Finnian caught sight of him — the familiar slump, the faraway stare. Brooding again.

He couldn't have that.

Pushing off from the doorway, Finnian crossed the hall, boots echoing faintly against the stone.

"What's stirring behind that thick skull of yours?" he called, a glint in his eye. "Don't tell me you've started writing poetry."

Eldrin chuckled, the light returning to his eyes. Finnian always knew how to lift a moment.

"No poetry, I'm afraid. But there's a chance to show off your scouting skills tomorrow. Join me on a hunt?"

Finnian raised a brow. "Sure, why not. But what exactly are we hunting?"

Eldrin's smile faded just slightly. "Answers."

Chapter 8

Adrelf led Eldrin and Finnian through the stone corridors, their footsteps echoing faintly in the dim firelight. The air held the chill of old stone, touched with the scent of mineral and ash—remnants of the recent battle still lingering.

Thalendir followed a few steps behind, expression tight. He had said little since their return from the ramparts—only a dry, muttered comment about "babysitting elflings" when Lyria had instructed them to rest.

Eldrin had accepted Lyria's hospitality. He didn't want to seem ungrateful—and, truthfully, he hadn't meant to offend her. But clearly, he had much to learn about the drelves and their ways.

Before retiring, he settled the Elven warriors, posting a few as sentries and assigning the rest to small chambers carved from the rock. Thalendir offered no help, but barked quiet orders of his own, clearly annoyed.

The passage twisted through cool stone; the walls etched with winding patterns—ancient symbols that pulsed faintly with embedded minerals, catching the torchlight like veins of magic. Not quite tunnels, not quite halls, the drelf corridors felt both carved and grown, shaped over centuries with pride and purpose.

The chamber itself was small but solid. A low ceiling of dark stone arched overhead, and a narrow slit near the top let in a ribbon of moonlight. Wooden beams braced the walls, and a sturdy cot of carved rock and fur-lined bedding waited in the corner. On the shelf beside it sat a single clay basin and a small bowl of dried berries—simple, but intentional. Everything in the room had weight, purpose. No ornament for ornament's sake.

Thalendir sniffed. "Well. At least it's not a cave full of bats. I'll be in the next chamber—in case you need me to chase away the shadows, little brother."

"I don't need you to watch over me, Thalendir. I'm a grown elf, and I've proven I'm an excellent warrior."

Thalendir turned back, one brow arched. "Have you? Because from what I saw, you're still acting on instinct and impulse. Bringing a drelf into our kingdom. Defying orders. Now playing house in their mountain stronghold."

Eldrin's jaw tensed. "I made a choice. One that saved lives."

"Yes," Thalendir said coolly. "And it nearly cost you everything."

Silence stretched between them, taut as a bowstring.

"Why did you come anyway?" Eldrin muttered. "You had no reason to help me. Or them."

Finnian, who had been hovering near the chamber's entrance, rubbed the back of his neck. "Well… this feels like a great time to go check on my room," he muttered. "I'll just…"

"Stay right there, Finnian," Eldrin cut in, his voice sharp. "I want you to hear this."

Finnian froze, halfway turned, then looked down and fidgeted with the leather wrapping on one of his boots. "Right. Of course. I'll just… stand awkwardly over here, then."

Thalendir looked away, his expression flickering. "Because of a promise I made… a long time ago."

Eldrin frowned. "To whom?"

Thalendir's gaze lingered on the stone floor a moment too long—then he straightened, slipping the moment aside like a cloak.

Eldrin knew that look. It always came right before a deflection. A truth buried instead of spoken.

"I heard you two," Thalendir said, his tone lighter now. "Talking about the hunt tomorrow. I'll be joining you."

Eldrin blinked. "What? No! Are you spying on me now?"

Thalendir shrugged. "Call it strategic observation. If there's danger beyond these cliffs—and I'm sure there is—I'll need to be there. Someone has to make sure you don't wander off a ledge."

Eldrin shook his head, but a faint grin tugged at his mouth. "You just want to get out of helping the drelves."

"I do. That, and I want to see the lay of the land." Thalendir turned toward his chamber, then paused at the threshold. "I'm not asking, little brother. I'll see you bright and early."

With that, he stepped through the doorway, brushing hard against Finnian's shoulder—his cloak whispering against the stone as he vanished into shadow. He didn't look back—but his steps slowed, just once, as if some unspoken weight clung to his heels.

Finnian whistled after Thalendir's departure. "Edgy little fellow, isn't he?"

Eldrin huffed a quiet laugh. "Don't let him fool you. He's not all edge. There's steel under it."

Finnian arched a brow. "Yeah? Well, I hope his steel doesn't stab me in my sleep."

Eldrin smiled faintly and settled onto the cot, the stone surprisingly warm from the day's heat still trapped in the walls.

"Let's get some sleep, Finnian. It's been a long day, and the sun will rise earlier than we'd like."

"Right. Then…" Finnian said, his voice muffled as he turned to go. "Just promise you'll wake me, even if I'm still snoring? Wouldn't want to miss the hunt."

Eldrin chuckled softly, waving a hand at Finnian to send him off.

The footsteps faded.

Silence crept back in.

He lay on the cot, the warmth of the stone fading beneath him, the air still and dry as his hand touched the Aetherstone — still pulsing softly beneath the leather pouch.

Outside, the wind threaded through the peaks like a breath held in the dark.

He listened as Finnian's breathing in the next room settled into a slow, steady rhythm. His friend was already chasing dreams—of food or swordplay, no doubt. But for Eldrin, sleep hovered just out of reach.

The fire in the hearth burned low, casting long shadows across the carved walls. The Drelf Kingdom was still.

Somewhere in the dark outside his narrow window, a flicker of movement shifted—a scrap of shadow against shadow. A faint chitter, too soft to be wind, brushed the stone. Then nothing.

Eldrin's gaze lingered on the slit of moonlight until his eyes blurred.

And somewhere in that stillness—quiet, deep, and ancient—he drifted into a restless sleep.

Eldrin stood at the edge of the Revealing Pool.

But the water was no longer there; it was now silvered glass, frozen in perfect stillness. The stars blinked like watchful eyes, their light trembling on the mirrored surface. Each breath felt heavy, as if the world itself were holding it in.

Behind him, a soft glow stirred.

Gantar stepped from the shadows, cloaked in green and silver, his hand resting over the Aetherstone pendant as it pulsed faintly.

"The second mark is stirring," the old sage said quietly. "You feel it, don't you? The pull. The hum beneath the silence."

Eldrin nodded, though his lips would not form words.

"The next bearer is near," Gantar continued. "But knowing who—and being ready to see who—are not the same."

A hairline crack spread across the mirrored pool beneath Eldrin's feet, spiraling outward.

His hand dropped to the pouch at his side, where the Aetherstone burned warm against his fingers.

Gantar's gaze followed.

"The mark follows fire," he said. "But not all fire burns in plain sight."

The reflection shimmered… then shifted.

Eldrin looked down. In the silvered glass, he saw his own face… then another beside it. Shadowed. Familiar. Just beyond reach.

"The bearer stands close to destiny…" Gantar whispered.

Then the pool shattered.

Fractured reflections scattered across the surface—Eldrin's face splintered with them.

"Wait," he called out. "Is it me, Gantar? Am I the next bearer?"

But Gantar was gone.

Only the wind remained, curling through the broken dream like a whispered warning.

The Aetherstone pulsed once—sharp and warm.

Eldrin clutched it instinctively, heart pounding.

It couldn't be… could it?

But there was no answer.

Only silence.

Only night.

They woke in the same breath — bolting upright, worlds apart.

Across stone halls and sleeping chambers.

Across the kingdom.

The fire had burned low. No voices stirred. No breath but their own.

Lyria's hand flew to her throat as the mark ignited, casting pale silver light across her walls. At that same instant, Eldrin's eyes snapped open, the Aetherstone at his side pulsing in answer.

For a heartbeat, the world itself seemed to listen — suspended between light and shadow.

Then the glow faded, leaving only the hush of stone and ember…
And the prophecy, still trembling between elf and drelf.

Chapter 9

The first pale line of dawn had barely brushed the mountain peaks when Eldrin slipped from his cot. The hearth fire had gone cold, but the Aetherstone still throbbed faintly against his side, echoing the rhythm of his dream.

He'd woken more than once in the night, the image of Gantar's face over the mirrored pool clinging to him like mist. *The bearer stands close to destiny*... The words still rang in his mind, unanswered and heavy. Whomever the next mark chose—whether him or someone else—was no longer some distant truth. It was near.

He could feel it in the Aetherstone as it pulsed—warm, deliberate—as if in agreement. Or a warning.

Eldrin exhaled slowly, shoving the thought aside before it rooted too deeply. There would be time to wrestle with prophecy later.

For now, there was the hunt.

He moved quietly, boots soft on stone, not wanting to wake the others—though Finnian would never forgive him for letting him sleep through a hunt.

Eldrin paused at his friend's door and rapped softly. "Up," he whispered.

A muffled groan. "Tell me it's at least midday…"

"It's dawn. Let's go before anyone notices."

Boots scuffed, gear was slung over shoulders, and they slipped into the corridor—only for a shadow to detach itself from the wall ahead.

"Going somewhere?" His voice was low, almost amused.

Eldrin stifled a sigh. "You weren't invited," he said.

"And yet," Thalendir said, falling into step with infuriating ease, "here I am. Try not to look so disappointed."

They emerged into the bite of the morning air. Kaelis stood at the cliff's edge, her wings half-unfurled and catching the wind. Another drelf scout waited beside her, lean and silent, the sheen of their dark wings catching the dawn light.

On the stone terrace behind them, the elves' mounts waited, saddled and ready, breath steaming in the chill air—Steel, Thalendir's black stallion, pawing the ground with restless strength; Silverwind, Eldrin's silver-white mare, tossing her head as the wind teased her mane; and Embermane, Finnian's buckskin gelding, ears flicking toward the sound of beating wings.

Something small darted across the far edge of the terrace, quick as a dropped shadow. The horses shied, then settled, as if the thing had already slipped away.

"You're late," Kaelis said.

"We're early," Eldrin countered.

"Not early enough." Her wings flared in a sudden gust, a silent promise that she would not be the one slowing the pace. "Mount up — and try to stay with us."

Kaelis didn't wait for a reply. With one powerful sweep of her wings, she vaulted from the cliff's edge, the rush of wind scattering loose gravel across the terrace. The scout followed a heartbeat later, diving after her in a smooth arc that caught the dawn light along the curve of their wings.

Steel snorted, pawing at the ground as Thalendir took the reins and swung easily into the saddle. The stallion's ears pinned forward, muscles coiling, ready to lunge at the first command.

Beside him, Silverwind tossed her head, silver mane flashing in the light as Eldrin steadied her with a firm hand. She danced sideways, restless, sensing his urgency as though it were her own.

Embermane gave a sharp whicker, stamping the earth hard enough to scatter dust. Finnian grinned, adjusting his stirrups as the buckskin gelding shifted beneath him, impatient and alive with the promise of motion.

Three mounts, three riders — united by purpose, bound by unspoken tension — ready to ride into shadow.

"Well," Finnian muttered, tightening his reins, "nothing like a little intimidation to start the morning."

"Still think she likes you?" Eldrin asked.

"Of course." Finnian's grin was all calm confidence. "It's early morning. She just warms up slowly. By midday, she'll be laughing at my jokes."

"Or sharpening a blade," Eldrin said.

"Details," Finnian replied with a wink.

Above them, the drelves were already dwindling to specks against the pale sky, their silhouettes slicing through the dawn.

"Try not to fall behind," Thalendir called over his shoulder, smirking as he urged his stallion into a full gallop.

The others followed, hooves striking sharply against stone before pounding over the hard-packed earth of the mountain trail. The cold bit at their cheeks, pine and frost mingling in the air as the chase began.

For the first mile, they urged their horses on, pushing them hard in the thin morning air. But it was pointless — wings outpaced hooves with ease, and the drelves were gone from sight before the second turn.

"Seems our guides don't intend to guide much," Thalendir said dryly, though he didn't slow Steel until the trail narrowed.

By the third mile, the path plunged into a dense tangle of spruce and pine, frost clinging to the needles. The air grew heavier, the cold sharper in the shadowed wood. Hooves crunched over roots and damp earth as the pace dropped to a careful walk.

Somewhere ahead, Kaelis and her scout had vanished into the canopy—or perhaps they were watching from above, unseen.

The forest closed around them, muffling the rhythm of the horses' steps. Breath steamed in the cold, curling and vanishing into the half-light.

Somewhere behind them, something skittered over stone. So light it could have been a squirrel. So quick it could have been nothing at all. It was gone before Eldrin could turn his head, swallowed by the dark weave of trunks and frost.

Finnian slowed Embermane, scanning between the dark trees as Thalendir pressed forward through the brush.

"You hear that?" Finnian asked.

Eldrin did — a faint rustle ahead, like leaves brushing together without wind. His hand went to his bow. "Movement. There—"

A pale shape stepped into the gap between the trees.

It moved with the unhurried grace of something that had never known fear. Its coat shimmered like frost on moonlit grass, each step soundless over the frozen earth. Antlers swept wide, catching silver glints in the dim light — not metal, but something older, more alive.

"By the stars…" Finnian breathed. "What is it?"

Eldrin raised his bow, a grin tugging at his mouth. "Breakfast," he murmured.

The animal stepped fully into the clearing, silver-dappled coat glowing faintly as the first light of dawn touched it. Breath plumed from its nostrils, and its spiraled antlers shimmered as though catching light from another realm.

It turned its head slightly, watching them with eyes like deep river water.

A rush of cold air broke the moment — Kaelis dropped from the canopy, wings flaring as she landed between them and the creature.

"Stand down!"

"What in the Vale—?" Finnian started.

"That," she said, voice like drawn steel, "is a Gladehorn."

The name landed with weight, though the two elves didn't seem to know why.

Finnian frowned. "Never heard of it."

"The Gladehorn is a Watcher of Balance. It appears when the realms are shifting. Some say they once walked beside the white dragons, before the Covenant was broken."

Her gaze cut between them, sharp as flint. "Spill its blood, and the land will not forgive you. And neither will I."

She stepped aside. The Gladehorn regarded her in silence … lowering its head in a slow, almost ceremonial bow before melting back into the trees without a sound.

The silence it left behind was different now—charged, as though the forest itself was holding its breath.

Branches crackled behind them.

Thalendir rode into view, Steel's black hide steaming in the cold. He reined in sharply, scanning the trees as if expecting danger.

"What was that?" he asked, eyes narrowing.

"A Gladehorn," Kaelis said.

"Why did you let it go?" asked Thalendir.

Eldrin's grip tightened on his reins. "Because it's not ours to take."

Thalendir's gaze flicked between Eldrin and Kaelis, suspicion darkening his features. "A fine prize walks into your sights, and you let it go? Tell me that isn't drelf superstition."

Kaelis's wings shifted, a subtle warning. "Call it what you want, prince, but you'd do well to remember this—some blood, once spilled, will stain more than your hands."

For a long beat, Thalendir held her gaze before giving Steel a sharp nudge forward, muttering something under his breath.

Finnian glanced at Eldrin, eyebrows raised. "And here I thought I was the one she didn't like."

Kaelis's wings folded tight against her back as she turned to her scout, exchanging a few clipped words in the drelf tongue. The scout nodded once and melted into the trees, moving with the ease of shadow.

She faced the elves again. "Since it's clear, you can't tell a sacred Watcher from supper, you'll take your lead from us."

Finnian raised both brows. "Then perhaps you can enlighten us. What *is* on the menu?"

Her eyes narrowed, but a faint, dangerous smile touched her lips. "Stoneback hare, frost grouse, or mountain stag—if you can catch them. They'll feed the hall without cursing the land."

Thalendir gave a short, humorless laugh. "Sounds more like a scavenger list than a hunt."

Kaelis's gaze cut to him, sharp and unblinking. "Better a scavenger than a fool who poisons the ground he stands on."

Eldrin inclined his head in silent acknowledgment, though his eyes flashed toward Thalendir. "We'll follow your lead."

"Wise," Kaelis said, already moving ahead through the undergrowth. "Try to keep up this time. And keep your arrows clean."

She disappeared into the shadows, the drelf scout's footsteps barely audible somewhere to the right.

Finnian leaned toward Eldrin as they guided their horses after her. "You hear that? She likes me enough to give me rules."

Eldrin smirked. "She's giving you a leash, Finnian. Try not to strangle yourself with it."

Behind them, Thalendir's voice cut through the cold air, low and edged. "Leashes are for hounds."

Eldrin didn't turn, but the faint twitch in his jaw said he'd heard.

A flicker of movement darted across the path ahead.

Steel's ears flicked forward, and Silverwind gave a sharp snort. Eldrin's hand went to his bow—then hesitated as a small, slender creature skittered from the brush.

It moved with startling speed, clawed feet blurring over the ground before it stopped a few paces ahead. Large amber eyes blinked at them from a narrow, foxlike face. Its hide shimmered faintly green and gold in the slanting light, bands of color shifting as it tilted its head. Its tail flashed upright when it stopped.

Beneath his tunic, the Aetherstone warmed—just enough for Eldrin to notice. The heat pulsed against his ribs in slow, deliberate beats, slightly out of sync with his own heartbeat.

"What in the—" Finnian started, leaning forward in the saddle.

The creature chirruped—a sound somewhere between a birdcall and a purr—then dashed a few feet farther, glancing back at them with unnerving focus.

Eldrin's fingers brushed the Aetherstone through the leather pouch. The pulse lingered, insistent, but his gaze kept drifting back to the strange little thing. Whatever it was, danger didn't seem to cling to it—if anything, it felt… inviting. He pushed the warmth of the stone out of his mind.

Finnian grinned. "Now that," he said, "is the fastest breakfast I've ever seen."

"Not enough meat on its bones to bother," Eldrin said, though his tone had softened. The little thing was oddly… charming.

Thalendir huffed. "We're here to hunt, not chase vermin. It's obviously not a… what did she say?"

"A frost grouse," Finnian answered without missing a beat.

Both brothers turned to look at him, surprise flickering across their faces.

"What?" Finnian said, feigning innocence. "Didn't you listen to her?"

Thalendir opened his mouth for a sharp retort—then stopped.

The skitterling had crept closer, head tilted, those amber eyes fixed on him. For the briefest moment, it froze, then gave a slow blink, its ears angling toward him in a strange, attentive way.

Steel shifted under Thalendir, but he didn't move. The little creature gave a quiet, warbling trill—almost like a greeting—then darted away again.

Eldrin caught the faint change in his brother's expression—not warmth, exactly, but the smallest easing of that perpetual iron in his gaze.

"Charming little pest," Thalendir muttered at last, though the words carried less bite than before. "I think it wants us to follow."

The skitterling's tail flicked once in the air, as if it had heard, and it bounded ahead with renewed energy, drawing all three of them deeper into the trees.

Without realizing how far they'd strayed, they pressed their mounts forward, the path narrowing as spruce and pine knit overhead. The air thickened, shadows pooling between the trunks. A thin veil of frost clung stubbornly to the ground here, untouched by the sun.

The Aetherstone throbbed again—two sharp beats, then stillness. Eldrin adjusted the strap of his bow, pushing the distraction aside.

The creature stopped just often enough to keep them close—head cocked, eyes gleaming with strange intelligence.

Finnian leaned toward Eldrin. "If Kaelis asks, we're rescuing it."

"From what?" Eldrin asked.

Finnian's grin widened. "Loneliness?"

Eldrin raised an eyebrow, but the little thing had already captured his attention—quick, sure-footed, and oddly… deliberate in where it led them.

It zigzagged ahead, weaving through roots and under low branches until it crouched low. Its tail twitched once, twice—then it darted to the side of the trail.

Finnian followed its movement—and saw them. Fresh hoofprints pressed deep into the damp earth.

"Deer," Finnian murmured. "Or, mountain stag, perhaps?"

The skitterling trilled softly, then bounded forward again, the sound swallowed by the hush settling over the forest. The light thinned further here, as though the morning had retreated behind the clouds.

They rode on, following its gleaming hide flashing between the shadows—never once glancing back to Kaelis's trail.

It led them between leaning pines and over a narrow rise where the frost held its shape in fragile patterns.

It paused again, tail twitching, then slipped toward a clearing where the pale light dimmed.

"Nearly lost it," Finnian murmured, urging Embermane forward.

Eldrin kept his bow ready, senses sharp.

Thalendir, silent now, nudged Steel to match their pace. "If it's guiding us to the game, we take it. If not—"

He never finished.

A hiss of air split the silence—then the world snapped tight. Weighted nets dropped from above, tangling limbs and pinning them hard against the cold earth. The fibers were rough and faintly stank of pitch, biting into the skin with every move.

Silverwind reared, Steel lashed out, and Embermane's whinny split the stillness—but more ropes fell, yanking them down.

Figures dropped from the trees—dark shapes with glints of metal and eyes like burnished glass. Shadows peeled away from the trunks, faces hidden beneath hoods, the gleam of curved steel catching the dim light.

Finnian froze mid-struggle, breath sharp. "I thought they were just… stories."

"What are they?" Eldrin shouted.

"Dark elves," Thalendir said, his voice grim.

One stepped forward, voice a low ripple, cold and smooth. "Welcome to the Arden, travelers. You've strayed far from your hunt."

Beyond them, the skitterling lingered in the pale rim of the clearing, head cocked, tail flicking once—almost like a farewell. Then it turned, vanishing into the undergrowth, leaving only the faint rustle of leaves… and for the elves, the sinking certainty that it had led them here all along.

Chapter 10

From the ridge's shadow, Drakor watched the nets fall. The dark elves moved with a predator's grace, cloaks swallowing the light, curved blades glinting like slivers of moon. He had set the snare, sent the lure that guided the prey into the perfect line—and now the trap closed exactly as intended.

A flash of green-gold slipped from the undergrowth. The skitterling bounded up the rocks to his side, tail flicking in quick, proud arcs.

"Clever bones," Drakor murmured, smoke coiling from his nostrils. Satisfaction thrummed through his chest, the old rush of the hunt stirring in his blood. "You did well."

The skitterling chirruped softly, leaning into the warmth of his breath.

"We sought one," he said. "But I will deliver all three—more than promised."

Drakor's gaze never left the forest. "Go. Stay close to them." His eyes narrowed to slits of gold. "If anything threatens the prize, you'll find me."

The creature gave a quick trill and vanished into the tangle of roots.

Drakor lingered a moment longer, letting the image settle—nets falling, prey caught, no escape. Zyressa would learn of his success; the Umbrin would whisper of it. The hunt had begun under his claw, and the proof was now bound and helpless.

His wings shifted, leather whispering like distant thunder as he turned from the ridge. The alliance had doubted his worth. They would doubt no more.

A dull ache throbbed behind Eldrin's eyes before he could place where he was. The dark elves had dropped them like sacks of winter potatoes, and they were all reeling from the fall. His head was thick, every sound muffled by the thudding in his ears.

Leather cords bit into his wrists, cinched so tightly his fingers had gone numb. The smell of damp earth and strange resin filled his nose, each breath heavy with it.

Finnian stumbled at his side, his own bindings pulled so tight the cords had cut raw lines into his skin. "Still alive," he muttered under his breath. "That's… something."

Ahead of them, Thalendir was already on his feet, flanked by two cloaked figures. His hands were bound, but his spine was straight, chin high — defiance in every step.

The nightborn moved without a sound, their cloaks swallowing the light, eyes glinting whenever they glanced back. One carried Eldrin's dagger at his belt, the hilt gleaming like a trophy. Another had Finnian's twin swords strapped across his back — blades that had never left Finnian's side until now. Eldrin caught the way Finnian's jaw tightened, his eyes fixed on the weapons as if sheer will might call them home.

Somewhere behind, the muffled clop of hooves marked Steel, Silverwind, and Embermane, each led by shadowed hands into the forest's gloom.

The deeper they were driven, the thinner the light grew, until the day felt far away and the air pressed close, as if the forest itself were watching.

Something hard pressed Eldrin's side as the darkborn shoved them forward. The Aetherstone. Warm — faintly pulsing — just as it had in the forest, when he'd ignored its warning.

The Umbrin had taken every blade, every bow, even the smallest dagger — yet the Aetherstone remained, steady against his side. Overlooked… or left on purpose. He wasn't sure which was worse.

A flicker of green-gold slipped between two gnarled roots, threading through the shadows.

Its amber eyes met his — then Finnian's — holding them for a heartbeat before it flicked its tail and melted back into the undergrowth.

Finnian's lips tightened. "Lonely, huh?" he muttered.

Eldrin clenched his hands, testing the bindings, feeling the absence of his dagger as sharply as the cords that bit into his skin. The forest pressed closer still, swallowing their trail until even the wind seemed to hold its breath.

The path opened into a wide hollow walled by black pines. Fires burned low in stone pits, their light catching on curved steel and pale masks. Dark elves moved in and out of the glow, some leaning against the roots of massive trees, others sharpening blades that never seemed to dull.

They shoved the three captives into the open space, forcing their shoulders forward. Around them, the ring of nightborn tightened — silent, watching. It was like standing in the center of a pack, every pair of eyes weighing whether to strike them or wait for a signal.

A tall figure broke from the ring. His cloak was deep violet; his eyes gleamed in the firelight. "So," Drovane said, his voice smooth and low. "The forest delivers more than promised."

From the shadows at the far end of the hollow, two massive shapes emerged.

Zyressa came first, scales glinting, her wings folded tight. She moved with a languid grace, but her gaze was sharp, sliding over the captives as if she were selecting from a feast.

Behind her came Drakor.

His talons dug shallow grooves in the frozen earth as he approached, the firelight catching in his twisted frame, the pale scars scoring his neck. He said nothing at first, simply circling the captives.

When his gaze reached Eldrin, it stopped.

"I said I would bring you the elf," Drakor rumbled, his gaze sliding to Eldrin before sweeping to include the other two. "I brought you three."

The nearest dark elves shifted subtly, proud of their haul.

Zyressa was now coiled in a half-lounge atop a fallen trunk, her scales gleaming wetly in the fire's glow. One talon idly scored the wood as her eyes tracked him. "You always did like to overcompensate."

Drakor's lips curled in something just shy of a smile. "Perhaps. But tonight, my excess is to your benefit." His tail twitched once, sharply. He stepped closer to Eldrin until his shadow swallowed him whole. Recognition flared — the forest, the stolen dagger, the drelf marked by prophecy. Smoke curled from his nostrils, and the slow curl of his mouth showed more teeth than smile.

Zyressa tilted her head, her voice a lazy drawl. "Pretty enough," she said, "but how do we know which one the mark has chosen?"

Drakor's tail twitched once, sharply. He stepped closer to Eldrin until his shadow swallowed him whole. "We test them…" he said, each word deliberate.

Velthar slipped from the shadows to join them. He shifted his weight at the edge of the firelight, the low scrape of claw on stone echoing faintly. Drovane's hooded face tilted, unreadable, but there was a flicker of approval in his stance — or perhaps anticipation.

Chapter 11

The forest swallowed all but the faint hiss of Kaelis's breath. She kept low, gliding between the roots of black-barked pines, every step placed with the care of a hunter. Beside her, the drelf scout moved just as silently, eyes locked ahead.

Through the tangle, a pale glow flickered—the faint light of a fire beyond the trees. Voices bled through the shadows, low and sharp, their words lost but their tone unmistakable: command, not conversation.

Kaelis eased forward until she could see the camp.

The captives were there—all three elves, bound and kneeling in the dirt, their weapons nowhere in sight. Eldrin's head was up, jaw set, even with the bruises darkening his face. Finnian shifted uncomfortably at his side, his twin sword-belts gone, wrists raw from the cords. Thalendir was still, shoulders rigid, the only sign of his anger in the slight flare of his nostrils.

She saw them before she saw the surrounding danger.

The dark elves were shadows draped in flesh—slipping between tree and firelight so smoothly it made the camp seem alive with its own shifting shapes. And then she saw what the shadows guarded.

A massive green shape lay coiled just beyond the fire's edge, scales catching the light in rippling patterns. The sheer weight of her presence pressed against Kaelis's ribs, forcing her to breathe slowly with shallow gasps. Across the clearing, a darker, leaner dragon prowled—his crooked wings stretched slightly, head tilted in a way that spoke of confidence and possession.

Her gaze caught on a smaller flicker of movement near his claws.

A skitterling.

It sat prim as you please on a rock, tail curling in neat, pleased arcs. The shimmer of its hide flashed once in the firelight before it hopped down and vanished toward the roots.

Kaelis's jaw tightened. A *skitterling?* She wanted to spit the words aloud, but kept them to a whisper. "Stupid elves," she muttered, more to herself than the scout. "How could they fall for that?"

The scout gave her a sidelong look, brow furrowed. "What now?"

Her eyes stayed locked on the camp. Her pulse was already hammering.

The darker dragon leaned in, his shadow stretching long over Eldrin. The tail twitched once. And somewhere in that indistinct murmur between them, Kaelis felt the forest grow colder.

The scout's voice was barely a breath. "We can't take them here. Not alone."

Every instinct in her screamed to move, to act, to drive a blade through the smug curl of the dragon's mouth. But she knew he was right.

What was she going to tell Lyria? Her friend had trusted her with the elves. She was supposed to take them out for a hunt, keep them safe, and occupy them for a bit. Now all she could do was watch them become the prey… and hope she wasn't already too late.

The darker dragon prowled closer to the captives. His tail slid across the dirt in a slow, deliberate arc before curling around Eldrin's middle like a noose. With one flick, he yanked the elf upright, boots scraping the ground.

Even from the cover of the trees, Kaelis saw his head snap back from the force. The dragon lifted him just enough that his toes barely touched the earth, holding him there as though weighing whether to crush or keep him.

Eldrin didn't struggle—not outwardly—but Kaelis caught the taut line of his shoulders, the way his hands curled into fists against the bindings.

The dragon leaned in, teeth bared in something that was not a smile. His torn wings shifted, casting jagged shadows over the firelight.

Kaelis's heart kicked hard against her ribs. She could face drelf council chambers, guard patrols, even shadow-born beasts from the outer ridges without flinching—but this… this was something else entirely.

The bright green dragon's head lifted from where she lay coiled, one golden eye opening to watch. Even that slight movement seemed to shift the air.

The drelf scout at Kaelis's side exhaled slowly. "We need to move. Before they discover us."

Kaelis swallowed, forcing her attention from the captives. They had caught five hares earlier. She stared at the lifeless game slung over the scout's shoulder—a poor excuse for what they would bring back.

Her pulse hammered as she backed away, one step at a time, until the firelight was nothing but a dim shimmer through the trees.

Only when the Arden's shadows swallowed them whole did she breathe again.

"Straight to Lyria?" the scout asked.

Kaelis didn't answer right away. She kept her eyes on the path ahead, though the image of Eldrin hanging in the dragon's grip burned in her mind.

"Yes," she said finally. "And if we're lucky… she won't skin ***us***."

Chapter 12

The council chamber was colder than usual. Not from the tall windows—those were shut tight—but from the weight of too many eyes watching her.

Lyria kept her chin high, meeting each gaze: Elder Maevric with his pinched mouth and ever-present doubt, Nyxari with her unreadable stare, and the others scattered around the half-circle of carved stone. Their voices had tangled all morning in debate—how many guards to post, whether to risk opening the outer gates for supplies, whether the darkness would strike again.

She had argued for action. They had argued for caution. And so, the air thickened with stalemate.

Nyxari's voice broke through the low rumble. "The omens grow restless," she warned. "Shadows gather—"

The door burst open.

Every head turned as Kaelis strode in, feet scattering a trail of mud, her braid torn loose, a hunter's bow still in her hand. Behind her, the drelf scout hesitated only a heartbeat before stepping in, bowing to the elders.

Kaelis didn't bow. Her eyes locked on Lyria.

"They have them," she said.

The chamber fell silent.

Lyria's fingers tightened against the stone table. "Who?"

Kaelis's voice came sharp, as an arrow loosed at full draw. "The elves. Eldrin. Finnian. Thalendir. Taken in the Arden… by the Nightborn."

A sharp intake of breath moved through the chamber—some of disbelief, some of dread. Generations had passed since anyone had seen the Nightborn, and drelves only spoke of them in half-forgotten warnings.

Kaelis continued. "And they were not alone. There were dragons with them."

This time, the murmurs rose in a wave, low and urgent, voices overlapping in alarm.

"Impossible," one elder said. "An old alliance… it cannot be," another muttered. Maevric's thin lips tightened. "Darkness rising."

Lyria rose to her feet. "What alliance?"

Nyxari's gaze swept the room. "Long ago, the Nightborn and the black-scaled dragons forged a pact—shadow and fire, bound for conquest. It was thought broken when the Nightborn vanished. If it stirs again…" She let the words hang, their weight filling the silence.

"They are in grave danger," Kaelis said, reclaiming the room's attention. "If we don't act, they will not survive."

"They are only elves," Maevric replied, voice dripping with disdain. "Why risk drelf lives for outsiders—outsiders who may not return the favor?"

"They fought beside us," Lyria shot back. "They bled here. That makes them allies."

"Allies until they turn," Maevric countered. "And you would drag our warriors into the Arden, to pit them against the Nightborn and dragons alike?"

Nyxari's eyes found Lyria again. "If the omens are true, the second mark will fall on an elf," she breathed, but her voice cut through the noise. "Perhaps even one of these captives." Her eyes scanned the council members. "Would you risk letting it fall into the wrong hands—into their hands?"

Silence.

"I'm going after them," Lyria said at last, the words ringing like drawn steel as her eyes swept across the room. "With or without your blessing."

Kaelis stepped forward. "And I'm going with her."

A few elders shifted in alarm, but Nyxari only inclined her head. "Send them with reinforcements... or prepare to account for the losses."

Lyria pushed back from the table, the scrape of stone loud in the quiet. She was already halfway to the door when Kaelis fell in beside her, the scout shadowing their steps.

The council voices rose behind them, angry and fearful, but the door closed on them all.

In the dim corridor, Lyria didn't slow. "Gather what you need," she told Kaelis. "We leave in an hour."

Kaelis caught Lyria by the arm before she could storm past. "Not like this," she said, voice low but unyielding. "You'll get yourself killed—and anyone with you."

Lyria wrenched free, eyes burning. "How could you let this happen? How could you let them be taken?"

Kaelis flinched as if struck. Her fingers worried the strap of her quiver; she would not meet Lyria's stare. "Don't—" she began, then forced the words out. "That's not fair. I didn't mean for this to happen."

"Then what?" Lyria demanded. "You don't like him — you made that clear. You don't like the idea of us— did you lose them on purpose?"

Kaelis's mouth tightened. "No. I swear. They were close together and then—" She broke off, breath catching. "I looked away for a heartbeat, and they were gone. I should've noticed. I should've been watching."

The corridor held its breath. Kaelis's voice dropped to something rawer, smaller. "I will fix this. I'll get them back."

Her eyes flashed up, not with challenge now but with iron. "I swear it."

Lyria's anger faltered; for a second, something like grief passed behind her eyes. Then she nodded, hard and fast. "Then let's move. Every moment we waste—"

"—is a moment to think," Kaelis cut in, stepping into her path. "The Nightborn don't keep prisoners out of kindness. They want them alive for now. They may torture them, but until they know for sure if one of them bears the next mark, they won't kill them. And the Umbrin are not alone out there—I saw at least two dragons."

The drelf scout shifted uneasily nearby, the leather strap of his quiver creaking under his grip. "We'll need more than speed to get them out alive."

Lyria's jaw tightened. "So, what's your brilliant plan?"

Kaelis didn't blink. "First, we learn their patrol routes. When they come and go, find any weakness. Then we strike when they least expect it. You care for Eldrin—I get it. But caring doesn't win battles. Precision does."

For a moment, Lyria said nothing, her breathing sharp in the dim corridor.

Kaelis leaned closer, her voice softening, though her eyes stayed hard. "I'm not asking you to wait. I'm asking you to make sure we all come back."

Lyria's gaze flicked to the scout. "Tell me what you know?"

The scout pulled a worn scrap of parchment from his satchel and unrolled it. The ink was rough, drawn in haste, but the details were clear enough—trees marked with quick slashes for height, a ridgeline where the Arden's canopy broke, the jagged outline of a camp ringed by spiked barricades.

"They've set up here," he said, pointing to the clearing between two ridges. "Shadows move constantly—in pairs. They've got watchtowers woven into the trees, and I counted at least a dozen of the Nightborn. Maybe more in the shadows."

"And the dragons?" Lyria asked.

The scout's mouth tightened. "Two… at least."

Lyria felt a cold thread wind down her spine. Old tales whispered of dragons and Nightborn conspiring together, but she'd never thought she'd see it. Such alliances belonged to the darkest chapters of history—and to see them reborn now meant the shadows were rising faster than they feared.

Kaelis studied the map. "We can't go in through the main approach. They'll see us long before we get close. But here—" she tapped the ridge to the east "—the terrain drops into a ravine. The canopy is thicker, and the wind from the cliffs might mask our scent."

Lyria traced the line with her finger, the beginnings of a plan sparking through her anger. "We could get close without being seen."

Kaelis nodded. "They'll expect us at night," she said.

"So, we attack during the day. Get the captives out while the dragons are sleeping…" smiled Lyria.

Kaelis's mouth curved—half approval, half warning. "Now you're thinking like a hunter."

The scout glanced between them. "We'll need at least twenty fighters. And someone to hold the ridge in case things go wrong."

Lyria exhaled slowly, forcing her pulse to steady. "Then we gather our best warriors. Quietly. No one on the council needs to know until we're already gone."

Chapter 13

The wind had changed.

Gantar paused on the narrow bridge of roots spanning the stream, his hand tightening around his staff. The Aetherstone at his chest pulsed once—faint, but steady—like a heartbeat felt through stone.

Eldrin.

It was not a voice, but a pull in his bones—the way the tide knows when the moon calls. He closed his eyes, letting the sound of the water fade beneath the hush of the forest. Threads of magic brushed against him—thin, frayed, and not all friendly.

Shadows moved at the edge of his mind. Wings like torn banners. The hiss of steel. A whisper in a language older than either elf or dragon, curling around him like smoke. The air tasted of iron and ash.

The Aetherstone flared again, sharper this time. *Pain. Restraint. A warning.*

Gantar drew a slow breath, steadying himself against the tremor that ran through him. Somewhere, a web had closed around Eldrin—and it would not be easy to break. And there, behind the pull, another shape loomed—distant but unmistakable. Dark. Scaled. Watching.

He opened his eyes. The stream whispered on as though nothing had changed, but the old sage knew better.

He turned toward the path leading back to his cottage. If the Aetherstone spoke true, time was thinning around them all. And if the omens he'd read in the old scrolls were right… Eldrin was not alone in what hunted him.

The forest leaned close as he walked, branches knitting overhead until the light was little more than fractured gold. Each step seemed to press deeper into something ancient—a silence that was not empty, but listening.

The Aetherstone pulsed again, and with it came an image—not a vision, but the ghost of one. Lyria, wings furled tight, eyes burning with a purpose that could scorch friend as easily as foe. She was moving quickly—away from the council halls, toward danger.

He frowned. She had heard. She would act.

The sage adjusted his staff and lengthened his stride. The wind had turned for a reason, and if he moved swiftly enough, he might discover what it was before it was too late—for any of them.

Behind him, the forest stilled. The breeze died.

The Aetherstone gave one final pulse—cold and dim—

As if bracing itself for the storm to come.

Chapter 14

The air in the Nightborn camp was heavy with cold ash and resin, thick enough to sting the back of Eldrin's throat. Above the warped tree line, a sun struggled against a canopy that swallowed most of the light, turning the world into a dim, green-black twilight.

He hung suspended in a cage of blackwood and bone, its bars slick with an oil that reeked faintly of iron. Below, shadows shifted—Nightborn sentries paced with the slow, predatory ease of creatures who feared nothing.

Across the clearing, Finnian's cage hung higher than his. The weight of captivity dragged his shoulders forward, but even from a distance, Eldrin could see his friend's eyes moving, sharp and restless, counting guards, marking escape routes no one could yet take.

Thalendir's cage was lower, closer to the firepit where smoke curled into the canopy. He sat motionless, gaze locked on the distance as if ignoring the dark elves entirely might somehow make them vanish.

The camp itself was ringed with spiked barricades woven from living trees, their branches bent and fused by old magic. From the deeper dark beyond the watch fires, the twisted dragon emerged—its scales blackened and warped.

At Eldrin's hip, hidden beneath the folds of his tunic, the Aetherstone stirred—its warmth pulsing like a heartbeat against his side.

Not now, he thought, forcing the air from his lungs in a slow, steady rhythm. The stone was their only hope, but if it flared now—if the dragon sensed it—they were finished.

A tremor rippled through the clearing, so slight it could have been a shift in wind. Across the shadows, the dragon's head lifted. One wing flexed, scattering embers into the air. Its eyes narrowed—slit pupils honing on Eldrin's cage.

The Aetherstone's pulse quickened, desperate and bright. Heat built beneath his palm, wild and alive. Eldrin pressed his hand flat over the light, every muscle rigid, commanding his pulse to still.

Breathe. Become the stone. Be unseen.

The glow dulled, sinking back into silence. The warmth ebbed to a faint thrum, hidden beneath his restraint.

Air rushed back into his lungs. His vision steadied.

The dragon's gaze passed over him, unseeing.

Only then did Eldrin dare to move—one heartbeat, one breath at a time.

Drakor's nostrils flared, the tip of his tongue tasting the air. Whatever he had sensed was gone. His head lowered, gaze sweeping past Eldrin.

The dragon moved with a predator's patience, its scales catching only the faintest gleam of firelight. But it was not his presence alone that made the air tighten—it was the figure walking beside him. A tall Nightborn, hood thrown back to reveal hair white as frost and eyes like two shards of obsidian.

"Three elves," the Nightborn murmured, his voice almost curious. "Where should we start?"

Drakor's grin was thin, knowing. "The prophecy speaks of another mark," he said, his voice carrying in the stillness. "Awakening in the blood of a forest-born. I think we should start with their blood."

At his signal, two Nightborn stepped from the shadows, carrying a shallow basin of glassy black water. Even the firelight seemed to recoil from it, shadows curling thicker around its surface. They dropped a sprig of twisted black vine in.

Thalendir's hands tightened around the bars of his cage. "You think to learn the prophecy's secrets with a cup of poison?"

Drakor's gaze slid to him, slow and deliberate. "Not poison. Truth."

"Shadewater," Drakor said, circling. "It drinks the truth from blood and shows what lies hidden."

Finnian's brow furrowed, and he swallowed hard. He glanced at Thalendir, then Eldrin. *What were they in for?*

Drakor's grin widened. "And if the mark sleeps in one of you… It will wake."

A faint hiss rose from its surface, as though the water itself breathed.

The smell reached Eldrin—metallic, sharp, and wrong.

The Nightborn set the basin upon a stone plinth, stepped back, and bowed their heads in something that felt too close to reverence.

Drakor's eyes scanned the three of them. "Who will be first?"

A guard stepped forward with a thin, hooked blade. "A drop of blood," Drakor said, his gaze locking on Eldrin. "Let's start with this one…"

Eldrin felt the Aetherstone pulse—faint, hidden—but the shock of it rattled him. He thought for a heartbeat that he heard Gantar's voice somewhere far off, like a whisper through deep water.

Ropes groaned as the pulley creaked, lowering his cage toward the ground. The bars swayed, rattling against each other until his boots scraped dirt.

The hooked blade gleamed in the firelight.

Eldrin's pulse beat fast. Every instinct screamed to fight—to kick the guard back, to make them work for every step. But the Aetherstone's faint thrum beneath his palm was steady, deliberate, as if urging him to hold.

Drakor's grin deepened, as if he could see the war inside him. "Struggle, and I will take more than a drop."

The guard reached for the latch. Eldrin's fingers curled into fists, his breath hissing between his teeth. He made himself steady—fighting would be futile. *What if I bear the mark? What will happen to me then?*

The latch clanged open. Cold air knifed through the narrow gap as the guard swung the door wide.

Eldrin stepped down, the leather straps biting into his wrists with every movement. Drakor loomed close now, his shadow stretching long across the dirt.

"Hold him," the dragon hissed, and two Nightborn closed in, their grips like iron on his arms.

The hooked blade hovered at his forearm. Eldrin forced his breathing to slow, even as his mind raced. *If the mark is mine…. how will they know?*

Instead, the blade pricked his finger. Eldrin did not flinch as a single drop fell into the basin. Then another and another…

The water shivered.

For an instant, starlight seemed to bloom beneath the surface—subtle, fleeting, but enough. The Nightborn's eyes narrowed in interest.

Drakor leaned in, molten eyes fixed on the faint shimmer. "Interesting…"

The glow winked out, swallowed by black water.

"Again," he ordered. "But this time, take more."

The hooked blade shifted toward Eldrin's hand, but then angled higher, toward the soft flesh of his forearm. The Aetherstone pulsed once—sharp, insistent—as if warning him that the next drop might cost more than blood.

"Hold him," Drakor hissed.

The dark elves tightened their grip until Eldrin's shoulders burned. He bit back a curse, the leather grinding against raw skin.

The blade's tip pressed in, drawing a thin line of red. The cut was long this time, enough for the blood to drip in a slow, deliberate stream into the waiting basin.

The Shadewater convulsed.

The black surface broke with a ripple, and light—faint but steady—spiraled outward from where the blood struck. Threads of silver coiled like smoke beneath the water before fading once more into darkness.

The Nightborn murmured to each other, the sound like dry leaves scraping in the wind.

Drakor's gaze never left Eldrin. "Something sleeps in you, forest-born… and I think I'd like to see it wake."

They took away the basin. Eldrin's heart thudded.

They shoved him back in the cage after cutting the bands around his wrists and flung a filthy leather band at him for his gaping wound. The faint silver spirals in the water clung to his mind, curling until they bled into something else.

His dream.

The one he'd had the night before.

He was standing at the Revealing Pool again, the surface like silvered glass, stars trembling across it.

The mark follows fire, Gantar had told him, his gaze deep and unyielding. But not all fire burns in plain sight…

Now, in the Umbrin camp, that image returned with blinding clarity.

Eldrin swallowed hard, forcing his expression into stone. The Aetherstone lay cool once more, but he couldn't shake the feeling that the silver spirals in the Shadewater had recognized him.

From the shadows, Drakor smiled. The taste of first blood was in the air.

Chapter 15

The moon was a pale smear behind the clouds, its light broken and thin. Lyria waited at the south wall for her friend, thrumming her clawed fingers on her forearm with impatience.

"You're late," Lyria said when Kaelis showed up a few minutes later. "I have summoned our fiercest warriors. They are ready to strike out as soon as I give the word."

"I'm ready," Kaelis replied flatly, scanning the shadows along the wall. "But if you want a chance of rescuing them alive, we go to Nyxari first."

Lyria's wings flared slightly. "We don't have time for detours."

"This isn't a detour," Kaelis said, stepping in past her. "It's the only way we make it back with them—and without the Nightborn tracking us before we reach them."

Kaelis strode forward without looking back. She knew Lyria was still standing there, stubborn and proud.

"We'll need more than a sword and a temper, Lyria!" she called over her shoulder. "And if you can't see that, then go ahead, get everyone killed."

The path to Nyxari's chambers wound along the cliffside, where the wind clawed at their wings. The Veilkeeper's door was unmarked, carved into the rock itself, a curtain of woven silver strands swaying in the draft. Kaelis pushed it aside without hesitation.

Inside, the air was thick with the scent of sage and rain-wet stone. Scrolls lay scattered across a low table, their ink still damp.

A whisper stirred behind them. Nyxari stepped through the curtain, her eyes catching the lamplight like frost. She looked between them as though she'd walked this path in a dream already.

"I knew you would come," she breathed. "The council was too busy arguing to hear what mattered." She set her hand lightly on the scrolls.

Kaelis stepped forward, Lyria a few steps behind her, but Nyxari lifted a hand. "Do not ask me to tell you which elf the mark has chosen. That is already in motion. The mark hides from all eyes, even mine, until it appears."

Kaelis's jaw tightened. "Then we need any help you can offer. To free them."

Nyxari's gaze flicked to Lyria, then back to Kaelis. "You will need Shadowcloaks. And as much power as we can summon." She moved to the far side of the chamber, her fingers brushing across the carved runes of a low chest. The symbols shimmered faintly, reacting to her touch.

Lyria and Kaelis looked from Nyxari to one another, then toward the chest.

With a deliberate motion, she lifted the lid.

The lamplight seemed to vanish inside. Cloaks lay folded within, black as the void between stars, their edges blurring and shifting as though woven from smoke. For a moment, the chamber itself felt dimmer, the air colder.

The Veilkeeper reached in, lifting a cloak from the chest. The furred fabric seemed to ripple in her hands, the outline refusing to stay fixed.

Kaelis and Lyria eyed the strange garment and then one another.

"What is it?" asked Kaelis.

Nyxari held the cloak aloft, its shadows bleeding across her arms. "A relic of the first war," she said, her voice hushed but steady. "Shadowcloaks. Woven from the hides of beasts that thrived in darkness deeper than even dragons dared to tread."

The cloak shimmered faintly, as though trying to slip from her grasp. "They will hide you from sight. Blur your outline, mask your scent, and even still your heat. They allow you to pass through dragon-fire unseen."

She let the words settle before adding, softer, "But shadows are fickle. These cloaks drink from the heart. If fear, rage, or desire sets your pulse racing—the veil will flicker, and the darkness will betray you instead."

Her eyes were fixed on Lyria. "Your temper is fire, Ironwing. Control it—or the cloak will burn you surely as any blade."

Lyria's wings twitched, her gaze fixed on the cloak.

Cold bled into the chamber, not from the draft but from the pall, as if the shadows clung to living warmth and drank it away.

Kaelis's jaw tightened. "Then we move like hunters, not prey. Still hearts, still hands. Anything else is death."

Nyxari held the cloak out to Lyria, its black fur whispering like smoke between her fingers. "Try it."

Lyria took it without hesitation, though her eyes narrowed, weighing the cloak in her palms. The fur was cool, almost damp, as if shadows had sunk into the pelt long ago and never left. She swung it across her shoulders.

The effect was immediate.

Her outline blurred. The lamplight bent around her, swallowing her edges until even her braids seemed to vanish into the dark. For a heartbeat, she was there—then not, a smudge of night standing where she'd been.

Lyria's wings flexed unconsciously, her claws tightening against her palms. "By the Covenant…" she whispered.

Kaelis's eyes narrowed, studying the way the shadows bent. Even she, who had hunted in darkness all her life, could barely see Lyria. A grudging respect flickered across her face.

But the veil flickered, just for a breath. Lyria's outline wavered back into sharp relief as her jaw clenched and her heart stuttered with an image of Eldrin in pain, bleeding. The image flared brightly in her mind, and the mark on her neck glowed. The robe shuddered with her pulse, shadows unraveling at the edges like smoke torn by wind.

Nyxari's pale eyes snapped toward her. "Quench your fire—or the cloak will betray you."

Lyria drew a sharp breath, but the memory of Eldrin's plight pressed too hot against her chest. The cloak wavered, shadows tearing loose from her outline.

Nyxari's hand lifted, palm outward. Her voice was quiet, steady as the tide. "Do not fight your heart. Breathe with it. Let the pulse slow. Shadows feed on stillness, not struggle."

For a moment, Lyria resisted. Her claws dug deeper into her hands, wings twitching with the need to move. But Nyxari's gaze anchored her, cool as frost, unyielding. Her eyes lingered on the faint glow at Lyria's throat. "The mark steadies what the heart cannot," Nyxari whispered. Her eyes lingered a breath too long on the glow at Lyria's throat before she looked away. "But marks are not chains, Ironwing. Even they can break."

Kaelis crossed her arms, her eyes narrowing on the flicker of the cloak. "Use the mark if it works. But if it fails…" Kaelis's jaw hardened. "Then we'll see what kind of hunter you really are."

Lyria's mouth tightened, her teeth gritting as Kaelis's words bit deeper than she wanted to admit. The cloak wavered with her heartbeat, shadows fraying at the edges. She forced herself not to answer, though the fire in her chest burned hotter with every breath.

"Again," the seer said. "In. Hold. Let the fire settle. Out."

Lyria obeyed, if only to prove she could. Slowly, the burn in her chest softened. Her pulse steadied, each beat less frantic than the last. Her mark pulsed once, steady as a drumbeat in the dark, and the fire inside her obeyed. The cloak seemed to catch that rhythm, shadows folding tighter around her, as though her blood itself commanded them.

Nyxari's eyes flicked briefly to the glow at Lyria's throat, but she said nothing as she inclined her head, her expression unreadable. "Better. But remember—your rage is quick to rise. In the Arden, a single flare will call every dragon within a mile."

As the mark steadied, so did the cloak—its edges knitting as though they answered to her blood as much as her will. The shadows pressed closer, clinging not just to her body but to the rhythm of her heart, as though testing whether to serve her—or consume her. A dangerous harmony, but harmony all the same.

When her eyes met Nyxari's again, they burned—not with wild heat, but with tempered resolve. Her voice was low, hard as stone. "I'll master it. With the help of my mark."

Nyxari inclined her head, though her voice stayed cool as frost. "See that you do."

The cloak stilled, a second skin of dusk clinging to her frame. But Lyria felt the truth of Nyxari's words coiled inside her chest: one slip, one surge of fury—and the darkness would turn on her. For a breath, she thought the cloak itself tested her, tasting the heat of her mark, deciding whether it belonged to her… or she to it.

Lyria's wings flexed, the mark at her throat pulsing faintly, as though answering.

Kaelis tilted her head, eyes narrowing—not just at Lyria, but at the weight of the mark itself, already tallying the risks that came with it.

The room was utterly still; the only sound was the hush of dimness brushing stone. Nyxari's gaze lingered, weighing fire against restraint. Then she closed her eyes as though sealing judgment and turned away. Her voice fell colder than frost:

"The cloaks will hide you from eyes and flame. But for strength enough to face what waits in the Arden… old debts must be called."

Chapter 16

Smoke rose from the fires below, curling like serpents around twisted branches and clinging to the elves' skin, hair, and nostrils. Thalendir tried to cover his mouth as black soot found its way deep into his lungs. His enclosure hung lowest, forcing him to endure the onslaught.

The wind had picked up, sending tendrils of darkness toward the canopy. All three cages swayed in the breeze, the ropes groaning against the strain.

Eldrin gripped the bars, his knuckles white, sweat running cold along his temples despite the fire's heat. Beneath the filthy rag around his forearm, his wound throbbed. Dried blood caked it as white oozed from the wound. His head swam, the world tilting each time the cage shifted.

"Eldrin." Finnian's voice came low, urgent. He pressed against the bars of his own cage, eyes sharp now, stripped of humor. "Are you alright?"

"I'm fine," Eldrin lied, though the word rasped dry in his throat.

"You don't look fine," Thalendir said from the lower cage, his tone clipped. "You look like you'll collapse before the next guard change."

Before Eldrin could answer, a shadow shifted across the clearing. The air itself seemed to grow heavier.

The dragon prowled from the tree line. His molten eyes fixed on the cages, lingering on Eldrin. He inhaled once, nostrils flaring.

"The wound eats at him already," he hissed, a smile curling his jaws.

One of the Nightborn guards shifted his hood, eyes glinting. "Why not bleed him dry now and be done?"

Drakor's tail lashed, gouging furrows in the earth. "Fool. Not until the blood speaks." His voice rolled like thunder; every word sharpened with hunger. His gaze narrowed, locking once more on Eldrin. "If the mark hides within him, I will see it wake. Even if I have to peel it from his bones."

Finnian lunged against the ropes, his voice sharp and furious. "What have you done to him?" His teeth clenched, but the fury in his tone couldn't mask the fear buried beneath it.

Eldrin tried to speak, but his chest hitched. A dry cough rattled through him, black spots peppering his vision. His arm burned, the wound seeping again beneath the filthy rag, white streaks threading through the dried blood.

The dragon prowled closer, each step was deliberate, claws gouging the earth. His eyes narrowed on Eldrin, hungry, unblinking.

He inhaled, tongue tasting the air. The curl of his grin widened.

"Weakness," he hissed.

Smoke bled from the serpent's jaws as he leaned close, the cage trembling beneath his breath. His tongue flicked against the ropes as though tasting what it might be to bite through them. Molten drops slid down his maw, hissing when they hit the ground. Thunder rolled from deep within his chest, but then he drew back, cruel patience sealing the hunger in his grin.

Eldrin's vision blurred, the firelight swimming. The dragon's words pressed into him, heavy and certain, like iron sealing a fate. He sagged against the bars, breath shallow, chest burning.

Then—against his ribs—the Aetherstone pulsed. Once. Steady.

It throbbed again—cool, deliberate—cutting through the haze like a drumbeat in fog.

Eldrin's fingers brushed the stone, its faint glow seeping through his fevered skin.

For a single heartbeat, it surged—alive, defiant—before he forced it down.

Be still. Be unseen.

The light sank back into shadow.

The pulse faded, veiled once more.

He hung in the cage's slow sway, every breath measured, every muscle locked. Across the clearing, the dragon's eyes remained fixed on him—unblinking, patient—like a predator studying prey too broken to flee.

The fire blurred, faces doubling and twisting in the heat shimmer. For a moment, the cage ropes looked like serpents writhing around him, tightening with every breath.

Thalendir's eyes darted from Finnian to Eldrin, then back to the dragon. His voice cracked. "Stay with us, little brother."

"Eldrin! Say something…," Finnian hissed, gripping the bars until his knuckles bled.

"He's fading fast," Thalendir said, his voice wavered.

The dragon's grin was cruel and utterly patient. Eldrin shivered—not from fever this time, but from the weight of those eyes—watching, waiting, as if his sickness was only one more step in a game Drakor had already decided how to win.

His arm burned like fire beneath the rag, the sickness seeping deeper with every breath. He clung to the Aetherstone — one last tether — before the fever dragged him under, the dragon's eyes met his… the last thing to vanish.

The blackness swallowed him.

At first, it was only heat—cloying, suffocating—pressing against Eldrin's skin until every breath scraped raw. The fire's crackle bled into whispers, too many voices tangled together, speaking in tongues he half-recognized.

The stink of soot and blood shifted to something else: rain on stone, sweet and sharp, cutting through the rot.

Eldrin forced his eyes open—or thought he did. The world shimmered, water pooling where there had been firelight. Shadows bent into shapes, then blurred, until all he could make out was a figure below. An elves' outline, cloaked, her steps soundless across the silvered ground.

The smell of ash clawed at him, and for a heartbeat, he swore he was back in the cage, soot stinging his throat. Then the haze broke, and the silvered ground returned, unmarred, unreal.

Her hands lifted the hood slowly as her long, golden hair rippled in the light, too vivid for shadow, too soft for memory. Eldrin's breath caught. He blinked, then rubbed his eyes. Fever or not, she was there—the most beautiful being he'd ever seen.

But beauty had no place in this camp of ash and blood. The fever burned hotter, twisting her outline until it blurred—then sharpened again. Her steps made no ripples in the pooled water. There were no marks where her feet should have pressed. Eldrin blinked hard, but the ground stayed smooth as glass.

Her eyes caught his, the color of sapphires. They held him still, burning away fever and pain alike. His chest tightened, though he couldn't tell if it was longing or the sickness dragging him under. Her smile curved—as if she already knew the measure of him, as if she'd been waiting. Eldrin swallowed hard, though his mouth was dry. Was this a dream, or something that had chosen his fever to find him?

He blinked, certain no one else could see her—until Finnian's breath caught sharply nearby.

For a moment, Finnian thought a fever was playing tricks on him, too. When he saw her, his hands froze on the bars of his cage. She moved beneath him; her cloak trailing like spilled moonlight, hair gleaming gold in the fire's dull glow. The smoke curled away from her, as if the air itself bent to let her pass.

Finnian's chest tightened, something sharp and strange settling there. She was unlike any elf he'd seen—too flawless, too radiant. His first instinct was to speak, to call to her. But the words died in his throat. All he could do was stare as she lifted her face, and for an instant, he thought her gaze lingered on him. His pulse leapt, traitorous heat rising in his cheeks despite the cold.

For a long breath, none of them moved. The fire cracked below, sparks twisting skyward, but all sound seemed dulled beneath the weight of her presence.

"By the Covenant… ," Thalendir whispered, his voice raw, stripped of its usual iron as he laid eyes on her. His fingers clenched the bars until the ropes creaked. Her eyes shone, and for a heartbeat, Thalendir was certain they lingered on him—the heir, the one bred for command. His grip tightened on the bars, pulse quickening despite himself.

A Nightborn stirred at the fire's edge, head turning as if sensing movement. His hooded gaze swept the camp, then passed right through her—as if she weren't there at all. He turned away, resettling by the flames.

Her steps made no sound in the dirt, no stir in the smoke. Only the three elves seemed to see her, feel her, want her. The longer they stared, the harder it became to remember the stink of ash, or the weight of chains.

Somewhere beyond the haze, the dragon's gaze lingered, molten eyes like embers smoldering through smoke. The elves' gazes had shifted, their hearts stuttering in unison. A wicked smile curled his lips as the fire in his belly rumbled.

"Yes… let them hunger," Drakor thought, his molten eyes narrowing. "Let them fall…"

Chapter 17

The silence after Nyxari's words stretched, heavy as stone. The cloaks in the chest seemed to stir with the pause, fur whispering against itself like restless shadows.

Kaelis narrowed her eyes. "Old debts?" Her voice was sharp, suspicious. "You mean the oath?"

Nyxari turned, her eyes seeming older than the mountains themselves. "Yes. The oath sworn in blood and storm. Long before either of you was born, when the drelves first fled into these mountains, we were not alone. The forest giants of the deep Arden walked here, taller than trees, their voices deep enough to stir the roots. They had fled, driven from the Arden, hunted by the Umbrin until their forests bled with ash. It was our blood and steel that broke the pursuit. We sheltered them—and in return, bound them by oath to remember, should the day come when we called."

Lyria's mark flared faintly at her throat, as if it recognized the word—giants—and the weight of the promise bound long before she was born.

"Giants," she said quietly, testing the word. "I've heard of them… but never thought they were real."

"Then they still owe us?" Kaelis asked, her ears flicking forward.

Nyxari said softly, her tone warning, "They do. But remember, bitterness can repay debts as easily as gratitude. The giants do not trust elves, and they will not welcome your companions. If the oath is called, they will come—for you, for your bloodline, Ironwing. Not for them."

Kaelis's mouth curved, a hard smile without warmth. "Then we don't ask. We take what was promised."

The seer's gaze lingered, ancient and unreadable. "Be wary of how you claim it. Old debts are forged in blood. Call them, and they will bind you—until blood answers blood, and the chain breaks."

The chamber dimmed as the lamps hissed low. Only the faint glow of Lyria's mark and the cloaks' shifting dark remained.

For a moment, no one spoke.

Then Lyria straightened, wings lifting slightly. "Then we'll call them. Whatever it takes, I'll see the oath kept—and the elves freed."

The forest winds clawed at the shutters, rattling them in their frames. The groan of ancient boughs answered the storm above, like old sentinels refusing to yield.

Gantar sat in silence. The chamber was dark but for the glow of the Aetherstone shard resting against his chest. Its light pulsed faintly—out of rhythm with his own heartbeat.

He closed his eyes. The tether drew taut, threads of unseen magic brushing across his spirit as harp strings strained to breaking.

Eldrin.

The young elf's presence flickered—weak, fevered—as if something gnawed at him from within. The sage steadied his breath, forcing his heartbeat to match the pulse of the stone. *If Eldrin could feel that rhythm, it might anchor him.*

But then another thread coiled through the link—soft, silken… wrong.

He stilled, listening with senses older than his bones. It was not dragon fire. Not the foul breath of the Nightborn. This was subtler, winding like perfume through Eldrin's mind—beauty masking venom, comfort masking pain.

Gantar's fingers tightened around the shard. "No," he whispered, the word barely a breath. "Don't fall for her."

The Aetherstone flared once, sharp and bright. Flashes seared his vision—water shining like glass, a golden figure bending close, three heartbeats quickening in unison.

His breath caught. A buried line of prophecy rose from memory, cruel in its clarity:

Beware the light that dazzles,

For beauty weaves the snare.

When hearts are done and undone,

The mark's fire shall falter—

And ruin shall follow swiftly.

His eyes snapped open. The shard's glow dimmed, veiling itself as though retreating from whatever was reaching for Eldrin.

Slowly, the sage rose, his staff catching the dim light. Beyond these walls, the council would still be talking, still blind to what moved against them.

Far away, a new player had entered the board—cloaked in beauty. Cloaked in lies.

Gantar pressed the Aetherstone to his chest, his voice low and edged with storm.

"Hold fast, Eldrin. Whatever mask she wears, whatever warmth she offers—don't let her claim you."

Lightning flashed through the window, splitting the dark.

"Beauty is a snare," he whispered,

"and hearts undone bring ruin swift."

Chapter 18

The forest was a hush of ash and smoke. Embers smoldered low in the pits beneath the Nightborn camp, sending up thin streams that curled like restless spirits into the black canopy. From his cage strung high in the trees, Eldrin drifted between fevered dreams and shadowed waking, every breath sharp against the festering wound in his arm.

The Aetherstone pulsed faintly against his side—once bright, now little more than a guttering spark. He clung to it as if to life itself, yet still the fever dragged him down, heavy and merciless.

A whisper brushed his ear.

"Eldrin."

His eyes fluttered open, and for a heartbeat, he thought the fever had conjured another vision. But she was there—leaning close, golden hair spilling like molten firelight, eyes like twin sapphires that pierced the gloom.

Cool fingers touched the wound on his forearm, and the burning throb eased.

"Peace," she murmured, her voice soft as a lullaby. "Be still. Gantar sent me."

The name broke through the haze. "Gantar…?" His throat was dry; his voice broken.

"Yes. He knew you were in peril. He sent me to heal you." She drew a small vial from beneath her cloak, its liquid glinting faintly blue. With deft hands, she pressed the mixture against the ragged cut. At once, the fire of the Shadewater eased into a dull ache. Relief washed over him, leaving him weak yet yearning for more.

"Who—" He swallowed hard. "Are you?"

She smiled faintly, as though the question amused her. "Carmyra." Her name shimmered in the air like a spell. "A friend."

She did not glance toward the other cages, where Thalendir's breathing was steady and deep, or where Finnian lay slack in restless sleep. Her entire being seemed drawn to Eldrin, as if he were the only soul alive in the forest.

"The mark called to me," Carmyra whispered, her eyes never leaving his. "Do you not feel it? The mark already stirs in your blood. That is why Gantar sent me."

Eldrin's chest tightened. Her words soothed and yet unsettled him, striking too near the fleeting shimmer he had seen in the Shadewater basin. *Could she know?*

Somewhere in his mind, Gantar's voice flickered like a fading echo: *Beware the light that dazzles, for in beauty the snare is set…*

The Aetherstone dimmed further as Carmyra leaned close, hair brushing his fevered skin.

"I will not leave you," she promised. "Until the fever has passed."

Her breath stirred against his cheek, sweet as honeyed wine, and Eldrin's resolve wavered. Even his pain seemed a distant thing beneath the weight of her presence.

From the next cage, an indistinct sound broke the spell—Finnian shifting, groaning faintly as though caught between sleep and waking. His eyes cracked open, glassy with exhaustion, and for an instant he saw her.

"Eldrin…?" he rasped, confusion thick in his voice. Then his eyes closed again, and he slumped back into uneasy slumber.

Carmyra did not turn. Her gaze remained fixed on Eldrin, her hand steady on his wound.

"Rest," she whispered, as though the word itself were a command. "When the time comes, you will rise. And I will be at your side."

The forest blurred into darkness. The weight of fever pressed heavily against Eldrin's eyes until, at last, he surrendered. Sleep claimed him swiftly, as if Carmyra herself had drawn the veil across his sight.

When he opened them again, the world had changed.

Gone were the cages, the smoke, the ache of wounds. He stood on a windswept ridge beneath a boundless sky, the air crisp with the scent of pine and freedom. She was there beside him, her golden hair tumbling loose, her eyes bright with joy.

She reached for his hand, laughter spilling from her like sunlight. "This is what life could be."

And it was. His fever disappeared, his arm healed, and the wound closed up, as though it had never happened. The Aetherstone at his side glowed steadily. A lightness filled him, as though he could run forever and never tire.

Carmyra drew him toward the horizon, where the land rolled into endless green valleys. The world unfolded around him in golden light. Eldrin stood on a grassy rise beneath a vast, clear sky, the air sweet with pine and wildflowers.

"Do you see?" Carmyra whispered, her hand warm in his. "No chains, no war, no oaths. Only freedom."

He turned in slow wonder. The forest stretched unbroken, green and endless, rivers gleaming like silver threads through the valleys. Far off, mountains shimmered white against the horizon. For a moment, Eldrin forgot the cages, forgot his captivity.

Then, the cries split the heavens.

His blood ran cold. Shadows swept across the hill as vast shapes wheeled in the sky—dragons, circling high above.

Their wings caught the sun, flashing bronze and gold, silver and sapphire.

Eldrin's hand went to his side, expecting to find a blade. He staggered back a step, heart thundering. "No. This—this isn't right. They'll destroy us. They always have."

Carmyra only laughed, as if his fear were nothing. "Look again."

And he did. The dragons did not dive, did not scorch the fields below. They soared in sweeping arcs, their roars not of rage but of triumph, echoing like a hymn across the sky.

Still, Eldrin shook his head. "They can't be trusted. I've seen what they do. I've fought them—bled because of them."

Carmyra's gaze was steady, her voice like velvet. "Not all dragons are enemies, Eldrin. Some long for more than war. For peace. For freedom. Just as you do."

He swallowed hard, his chest tight. The dragons were descending now, closer, their scales gleaming like coins in sunlight. He could see the strength in their wings, the wisdom in their eyes. And yet every part of him braced for fire, for death.

Carmyra leaned nearer, her hair brushing his shoulder. "Would you like to ride one?"

The question struck him like a blade between the ribs. He let out a short, incredulous laugh. "Ride? That's not possible."

"Is it not?" Her fingers intertwined with his, warm and certain. Then she lifted his hand and pressed it to her chest, where her heartbeat thrummed. "The mark calls you to more than battle. To more than chains and blood. It calls you here. To this. To me."

The heat of her skin bled through him, quickening his own pulse until he could scarcely tell where hers ended and his began. His breath came unsteady. Above them, the dragons wheeled, their shadows vast and solemn, drumming the earth in living thunder.

The wind shifted. One broke from the circling flight, its shadow sweeping across the ridge. It descended in slow, deliberate spirals, each beat of its wings stirring the grasses like a storm and thundering in their ears.

The shadow grew, swallowing the ridge in darkness. The beat of wings pounded like war drums in Eldrin's chest, rattling through his bones. His breath came ragged, his palms damp. He had faced dragons before—always with steel in his grip, comrades at his side, the certainty of death hovering close.

Now he stood unarmed, alone but for her hand in his, and the nearness of the beast stole all sense from him.

Carmyra's voice brushed his ear, low and steady. "Do not fear. If it meant you harm, you would already be ash."

Every instinct screamed to run, to fight, to do anything but stand waiting as the beast drew near.

The dragon alighted with a force that shook the earth, talons gouging deep into the soil. Its wings folded with a hiss of air, and for a heartbeat, silence reigned.

Sapphire scales, which matched Carmyra's eyes, shimmered in the sunlight. It peered at him—eyes clear, luminous—fixed on him.

Eldrin's breath caught. His hand twitched toward a blade that was not there. "It's a trick," he muttered. "They kill. That is what they are."

The dragon lowered its head, the ground trembling with the weight of its breath. Yet there was no fire, no hate in its gaze—only a deep, solemn watchfulness.

Eldrin swallowed hard, torn between terror and awe.

Carmyra's voice slid into his thoughts like silk. "Step closer. See what is possible."

His feet felt rooted. Every memory of fire and blood cried out to hold him back, yet her hand was steady in his, her gaze unwavering.

"One step," she urged, her voice soft as breath. "One step toward what the mark has promised you."

The dragon's eyes glimmered, vast and ancient, yet strangely patient. It waited—not predator, not foe—only watched.

Eldrin's throat tightened. The grass whispered beneath his boots as he shifted, and before he realized it, he had taken a step.

The dragon did not move. It only lowered its head further, as though in welcome.

Carmyra's smile deepened. "Do you see? The world is not what you feared. It is what I will show you."

The Aetherstone pulsed once against his side—sharp, warning—then dulled, smothered by the warmth of her hand.

And Eldrin, caught between awe and surrender, could not look away…

Chapter 19

The Arden loomed darker with every mile. Lyria moved like a storm barely contained beneath the hood of her Shadowcloak, her mark thrumming against her skin as if it knew Eldrin's peril.

Kaelis strode at her side, silent and fierce. Around them, their war-band moved in shadow, each bearing cloak and steel, the air thick with the musk of damp earth and coming rain. The forest seemed to resist them, branches creaking, roots clutching their feet, as though it remembered the Oath that was about to be called.

"Too slow," Lyria muttered. "He doesn't have time for us to creep. Where are they?"

Kaelis caught her arm. "Nyxari said they would find us."

Lyria jerked free, wings twitching against her back, the Shadowcloak flickering dangerously at the surge of emotion. The darkness recoiled, betraying her outline before she could master it again.

Kaelis's eyes narrowed. "Your mark burns too hot. If you can't control it, the cloaks will betray us all."

A heavy silence followed. Then the trees shuddered. A deep, slow rhythm, like thunder buried beneath the roots. The drelves froze, exchanging wary glances.

Kaelis's hand tightened on her sword. "The giants?"

Lyria's gaze swept the trees. "I don't think so…"

A low growl rolled through the dark. Then another. Eyes glimmered between the trees—red, narrow, and hungry.

"Panthers," Kaelis hissed.

The word shivered down the line of warriors. Their cloaks wavered as unease rippled through them, faint silhouettes flickering into view. The growls deepened, circling closer, threading the air with menace.

One of the younger warriors broke formation, his cloak trembling as panic set in. "They can smell us—"

A blur of shadow slammed into him before he finished. Fangs flashed, jaws snapping on fabric that hissed and smoked under their bite. The warrior cried out, stabbing wildly until Kaelis's blade struck true. The panther shrieked, dissolved into ash—then more answered its death cry from every side.

The war-band drew tight, weapons raised. Lyria's mark flared hot against her skin, her cloak flickering with it. She forced her breathing even, knowing rage would expose them all. Still, the mark burned, aching for release.

The panthers prowled low, tails lashing, muscles coiled to strike. Their growls thickened, vibrating through the soil. One lunged, then another — blades and spears clashed in a burst of steel and smoke. Two drelves went down hard, their cloaks flickering as claws raked across them. Kaelis barked orders, driving her blade through a throat that hissed and dissolved into ash.

Lyria swung her sword wide, cleaving a panther from shoulder to jaw. Its shriek rattled the forest, yet for every one that fell, two more circled in tighter. Her mark seared against her skin, the glow threatening to burst free.

Then the earth trembled.

A deep rumble rolled beneath their feet. Branches shook, leaves fell, roots split the ground. The panthers faltered, hackles rising, their burning eyes snapping toward the deeper dark.

But they did not flee.

Snarls turned to frenzied roars as they hurled themselves at the group with renewed desperation — as if sensing something greater was coming, and they meant to kill before it arrived. One slammed into Lyria's side, driving her back into the roots of an oak. Her blade caught it mid-lunge, but its weight bore her down until Kaelis's sword skewered it through the ribs. Smoke poured over them both as it dissolved.

"Hold the line!" Kaelis shouted, her voice raw.

The ground split with a thunderous crack. A tree groaned as something vast pushed through, stone skin grinding against bark. Ember eyes flared, red and terrible.

The panthers shrieked, their bravado shattering. Their eyes glowed, fixed on the rustling branches. For a breath, even the drelves thought the forest itself had turned against them.

Then…the panthers scattered into the dark, vanishing between the trees with tails low, the sound of their flight swallowed by the deeper rumble.

A giant stood before them.

The group staggered back as the colossus stepped into the clearing, each footfall shaking the earth. Behind it, more emerged — hulking forms peeling themselves from trunk and shadow, their faces carved of bark and stone, their presence heavy as storm clouds.

The panthers were gone. But perhaps the true danger was only beginning.

Lyria's heart hammered, not with fear but with the weight of choice. Old debts. Chains forged in blood. Nyxari's warning rang in her ears. Once called, they would not leave until they bled together.

She stepped forward, pulling back her hood. The mark glowed faintly on her skin. "Children of stone and storm," she said, her voice carrying through the hush of the Arden. "I call the Oath."

For a long moment, nothing stirred. The forest itself seemed to hold its breath.

Then the first giant bent low, its massive form blotting out the light. The sound of stone grinding echoed as its head turned, eyes locking on Lyria.

"Ironwing."

The name rumbled like an avalanche down the ridge, deep enough to vibrate in her chest. Lyria's breath caught. She had never spoken to one, yet it knew her, as if her blood carried the weight of memory.

Another giant stepped forward, bark splitting as its limbs straightened, a face carved of granite and shadow. "Long ago, your people bled for us. You broke the chains of the Umbrin and gave us shelter when we needed it most." Its voice was heavy, resonant, a storm bound in stone. "We made an oath to your kind. In blood. In fire. To come to your aid if ever you called."

The first giant's gaze shifted, sweeping over the gathered drelves. "And now you call it. But know this—we will not honor our oath until blood answers blood."

A murmur rippled through the war-band. One of the younger drelves shifted uneasily. Kaelis silenced him with a glare but kept her voice steady. "We fight to free our allies. Our blades will cut deep enough for both sides."

The giants did not look at Kaelis. Lyria was the sole focus of their attention, as if the mark upon her skin had already chosen her for the debt.

The leader's voice deepened further, stone grinding on stone. "Then let it be you. Child of oath and fire. Show us the blood you will give."

The ground trembled as the giant extended a hand the size of a house, its palm open, waiting.

Lyria's heart thundered. She felt Kaelis shift beside her, felt the war-band tense, but none moved. All eyes turned to her.

Nyxari's warning whispered through her memory: Chains forged in blood. Once called, they will not aid us until both sides bleed.

Lyria drew her blade. The steel caught what little light filtered through the canopy, gleaming sharp and cold. For a breath, she hesitated, the weight of every watching eye pressing down on her. Then, without flinching, she dragged the edge across her palm.

The cut burned hot, and blue-green welled forth as her mark flared. She clenched her fist, letting the blood drip into the giant's waiting hand. Each drop hissed as it struck the stone, as though the earth itself drank it in.

The leader rumbled low, a sound like mountains groaning. Slowly, he opened his massive fist, then drew a jagged nail across his own palm.

The gash opened wide, and molten light bled from the wound — not red, but deep amber, thick and luminous like fire trapped in stone.

He lowered his hand toward her. "Blood answers blood."

The war-band held still, silent as statues. Lyria raised her wounded hand, trembling only once before pressing it to the giant's.

Her blood mingled with his, blue, green, and amber fusing, searing where they touched. The heat lanced through her veins, sharp as iron and fire, until her knees threatened to buckle. For a heartbeat, she swore she felt the weight of mountains pressing into her bones.

Then the giant withdrew, lifting his burning gaze to the others. "The Oath is sealed. Your fight is ours until chains are broken, or blood runs dry."

The giants behind him struck their chests with stone-hewn fists, the sound rolling like thunder through the Arden.

Kaelis exhaled, her grip tight on her sword. "So be it," she murmured, though her eyes flicked to Lyria with something between awe and fear.

The forest itself seemed to shift, branches groaning as though the Arden remembered its old debt. Somewhere in the distance, a panther shrieked and fled.

But Lyria's palm still burned with the mingled blood, the mark on her neck thrumming in answer. She knew Nyxari had been right — chains had closed around her. And they would not break until the captives were free or all of them bled dry.

Chapter 20

Gantar sat hunched over his desk, the Aetherstone pendant cupped in his palm. Its glow was faint, unsteady — a guttering star at the edge of night. The chamber was still but for the crackle of a single torch.

He closed his eyes, reaching through the tether. A pulse answered, but it was weak, wrapped in something soft and cloying. Not fever. Not distance. A thread of sweetness masking rot.

His jaw tightened. Eldrin was slipping deeper, the stone warning him of danger. And beyond that thread, another weight pressed on him — Thalendir. For the first time since the brothers were elflings, the tether warned that both sons were falling into shadow.

If the council found out that the heirs were captured by darkness, they would circle like carrion birds. Whispers of weakness already stirred through the kingdom. He could not give them more.

But the king—yes, the king must know.

Gantar rose, his bones aching like old trees in the wind. He tucked the Aetherstone back against his chest, its cold bite settling heavily on his heart, and left his study.

The halls of the citadel were hushed, empty but for guards who straightened as he passed. He ignored their looks. His steps carried him unerringly to the king's chambers.

The door was unguarded, a rare thing. Eldermyst sat alone within, his silver-streaked hair catching the torchlight, his back turned to the great windows. His hands rested on the table before him, but there was no map, no scroll — nothing but the silence.

"Gantar," he said without turning. His voice was low. "You bear news."

The sage bowed his head. "I do. But not the news you would wish."

At that, Eldermyst turned, his eyes sharp as a blade. "Speak."

Gantar drew a slow breath, fingers curling around the stone at his chest. "Both your sons are in danger."

The words fell like an axe.

Eldermyst rose, the air shifting with him. For an instant, his composure cracked, worry flickering across his features before he mastered it. "The prophecy," he said, as though daring the world to deny it.

Gantar inclined his head. "I feel them through the stone. But something else entwines Eldrin and teases Thalendir — a snare. Sweet on the surface, venom beneath. I fear the prophecy itself hangs in the balance."

Silence stretched taut as a bowstring. The king's gaze drifted to the window, to the forest beyond. "The council will circle like vultures. They seek power, and if something happens…."

"You must not tell the council," Gantar said. His voice was firm, though soft. "This is not a matter for debate. They are your sons. Your blood. And more than that — the future of our realm."

Eldermyst's jaw tightened, his fists curling on the table. He did not falter. But the storm in his eyes was brighter than any torch.

Finally, the king spoke—low and resolute.

"Tell me, old friend. What shall we do?"

Gantar lowered himself into the seat opposite him, the firelight tracing lines of weariness across his face. "You must gather strength where the council cannot see," he said quietly. "Call upon those whose loyalty is to *you*—not to their titles, not to politics. And send spies. Find what ensnares them. Help set them free."

The king's gaze held his, searching for hope, for guidance, for meaning in the prophecy that still haunted his dreams. "Even now," Gantar continued, "Lyria and her fiery friend, along with her drelves and some of your own warriors, move to aid the captured elves. But they walk straight into the snare of dark forces—forces older and hungrier than you or I."

Eldermyst's jaw tightened. "And what of the mark? You think this second one truly exists?"

Gantar's eyes flickered, the shard at his neck pulsing faintly. "The balance shifts again, my king. The first mark awakened light. The second could either strengthen it—or undo it entirely."

The silence between them deepened, filled with the soft crackle of the hearth and the weight of unspoken fears.

At last, the king drew a long breath. "Then we cannot wait for the council's blessing. I will send my own."

Gantar inclined his head, a faint smile ghosting his lips. "Then there is still hope."

Eldermyst straightened in his chair, the firelight catching the silver in his hair. "Hope is not enough," he said. "If what you say is true, we'll need eyes in the dark and blades that won't hesitate. I will not risk open war until we know the full shape of what we face."

He turned toward Gantar, gaze steady. "You've already chosen who to send, haven't you?"

"I have, my lord," Gantar replied. "Caelith and Aelar—both loyal, both tested. Caelith is quick with a blade and quicker to anger. Aelar is steady, deliberate, and will temper the fire that drives him."

The king's expression softened slightly as he nodded. "Good choices. Quiet strength and quick steel—both will be needed."

Gantar's fingers brushed the Aetherstone shard at his chest. "They'll follow your banner willingly, my king. But what lies ahead may demand more than strength."

Eldermyst's gaze flicked to the window, where wind clawed at the shutters. "It always does," he murmured.

For a moment, neither spoke. The fire cracked softly, throwing restless shadows across the chamber walls. Outside, thunder rolled — distant, but drawing closer.

The king exhaled slowly, voice low but steady. "Strength alone won't bring them home. We'll need precision… and discipline." His eyes lifted to meet Gantar's. "Aerion. She'll serve well. Her aim never falters."

Gantar inclined his head. "A wise choice, my king. Calm where others burn too quickly. She'll steady them."

Eldermyst leaned back slightly, thinking aloud. "And they'll need a leader — one they trust, and one the council won't question should word reach their ears." A faint smile ghosted across his lips. "Master Trainer Aldareth. No one else would do."

Gantar's answering nod was slow, approving. "I thought the same."

The king's expression hardened into resolve. "Then it's decided. Send for them immediately. They leave tonight."

Gantar rose, the glow of the Aetherstone faint against his chest. "I'll see to it, my king."

Eldermyst's hand pressed flat upon the table, the firelight carving lines of iron across his features. His voice lowered, carrying both command and fear. "I will not lose both my sons to shadow. See that they return."

Gantar bowed his head. "As the king commands."

The king's gaze lingered on the flames, sharp and unyielding. "And, Gantar…" His tone dropped to a quiet edge. "Find those we can still trust. The council is already divided—and I will not let its weakness break this kingdom from within."

The Arden lay smothered under its canopy, the air heavy with smoke from the Nightborn campfires. Beyond the cages where the elves hung, two vast shapes shifted in the dark. Their scales glimmered faintly with each flare of firelight — one crooked and small, wings torn but quick, the other scarred and massive, her hide gleaming in the gloom.

Zyressa's laugh was a low, rumbling growl. "So simple. Not even a fight. He all but opened his veins for her."

Drakor slithered closer, his eyes gleaming. "Drovane was right. Their hearts betray them faster than any blade. A pretty face, a sweet voice, and they roll over. Elves are weak. Keen to be led by longing."

She bared her teeth in a jagged smile and turned toward the rogue dragon approaching. Velthar's scales shimmered a dull bronze, tarnished and rough as if scarred by centuries of battle. One wing bore a long tear that whistled when the wind caught it, and his eyes glowed with a hard, hungry light.

"What do you say, Velthar? About the feeble elf?" she asked.

His voice rasped, dry as bones scraping stone. "What does the prophecy say? You are certain he is the one?"

Drakor's gaze flicked to him, sly and secretive. "Certain enough to let her draw him out. If he bears the fire, it will show. And if not…" His crooked shoulders rose in a shrug. "We have two other elves to test."

Zyressa's wings shifted, scarred membranes catching the firelight. "And what if this one doesn't break? If he resists?"

Drakor's grin widened, sharp as bone. "Then the snare tightens. Doubt, desire, fear — all threads in the same net. He will struggle, and the more he struggles, the deeper he tangles. Either way, he is ours."

For a long moment, Zyressa watched the cages, her eyes narrowing. Eldrin stirred in sleep, lips moving as though whispering to someone unseen.

Zyressa's claws sank into the soil, the ground trembling beneath her weight. She exhaled, smoke curling from her snout. "Then let us hope the Umbrin's pet phantom earns her keep. I tire of waiting."

Drakor's chuckle was low, pleased. "Patience, Zyressa. The trap is set. And soon, the mark will burn bright."

Velthar's tail lashed once against the roots. "So, we agree, then? Once the mark reveals itself, we take it for our own. The Umbrin need not keep what they cannot hold."

A hush followed, heavy as stone. None of the dragons spoke further, but in the shadows beyond the firelight, a figure lingered. Drovane's eyes glimmered, sharp and knowing. Every word had reached him.

Chapter 21

Eldrin stood transfixed, his palm still burning where Carmyra had pressed it to her heart. The dragon's head bowed lower, vast and solemn, its breath stirring the grass in warm, steady gusts.

"She won't hurt you," Carmyra whispered. "As long as you are with me."

Her words wrapped around him like fine silk. The Aetherstone pulsed once — faint — then dimmed again, its warning smothered by the nearness of her touch.

The dragon rumbled, a sound deep and steady as the earth itself. Slowly, it lowered its wing, folding it like a stair of turquoise plates. An invitation.

Eldrin's throat tightened. He had fought dragons before — always with bowstring drawn, blade ready, every muscle taut with dread. To climb one? To trust one? It was madness.

And yet the thought of flight — of leaving behind chains, blood, oaths — burned in him like a secret he had never dared speak aloud.

Carmyra leaned close, her breath warm against his ear. "Come. Let me show you what freedom feels like."

She lifted her hand, and a length of braided gold shimmered into being, bright as spun sunlight.

With unhurried ease, she cast it over the dragon's horns and drew it taut, the rope gleaming against the dragon's scales. "There," she said, her voice light, as though the act were nothing at all. "Even the wildest storms can be tamed."

She climbed the dragon's wing, the rope steady in her grasp, her movements sure and graceful. Turning, she extended her hand toward him. "There is room for you."

Eldrin's throat tightened. No rope could tame a dragon. He knew this. Yet Carmyra stood radiant, fearless, as if she had been born to command such beasts.

His every instinct screamed no. But the thought of flight burned through him, fierce and tempting.

"Trust me, Eldrin," she whispered, her hand outstretched.

The Aetherstone pressed cold against his side, but its warning was faint, smothered by her nearness.

He swallowed hard, his heart pounding. The grass whispered beneath his boots as he stepped toward the dragon's lowered wing and reached for her hand. Her fingers closed around his, warm and certain, pulling him up. The dragon's hide trembled beneath his boots, heat radiating through his legs as he slid into place behind her.

Carmyra wound the rope once about her wrist, then guided his hands to her waist, her touch steady, intimate. "Hold fast."

The ground shook as the dragon coiled its limbs beneath it. Eldrin's breath snagged in his throat. Every instinct screamed to leap free, to draw steel, to fight for his life. His fingers tightened around Carmyra's waist instead.

Then came the surge.

The dragon sprang upward, the force slamming through him like a hammer. His stomach lurched, the world tilting into a blur of sky and shadow. Wind clawed at his face, cold and wild, tugging at his hair and cloak. He gasped, choking on the sheer rush of speed.

Wings spread wide — vast, thunderous — catching the air in a single sweeping beat. The ground dropped away in a dizzying rush. Trees shrank to toy-like shapes, the forest to a dark carpet. Smoke from the Nightborn campfires curled up toward them, faint and powerless.

Eldrin's heart hammered. He clung tighter, torn between terror and awe. Never had he felt so exposed. Never so alive.

Carmyra leaned back into him, hair whipping against his cheek, her laughter carrying bright over the roar of the wind. "Do you feel it? This is freedom, Eldrin. This is what we could have."

The terror ebbed, replaced by something sharper, fiercer. Laughter broke from his lips — raw, startled, alive.

For a heartbeat, he let himself believe it. This was freedom. This was what he had always longed for.

But then another face flashed in his mind — wings silver against the sky, eyes like amethyst burning with defiance. Lyria.

Now he knew what it felt like to fly. And the thought of how her broken wing had grounded her and what that must have been like struck him like an arrow to the chest. No wonder she had been so angry. So frustrated at having to ride instead of flying.

His laughter faltered. Guilt twisted through him, jagged and cold. *What was he doing?*

Carmyra turned her head slightly, her smile radiant, her voice soft, smooth. "Don't think of chains, Eldrin. Only me."

The Aetherstone gave a faint pulse — weak, but insistent.

Eldrin's grip loosened around her, torn between the fire of the wind and the whisper of stone against his side.

Carmyra's smile never faltered, though her eyes glimmered with something sharper than joy. She lifted the golden rope, guiding the dragon higher, until the clouds swallowed them whole. Mist tore past in silver veils, then broke — and transformed the world below.

They soared over valleys bathed in golden light, rivers gleaming like azure glass, forests lush and unbroken, untouched by axe or fire. Towers of white stone rose from the hills; their spires twined with flowering vines. Birds of impossible colors wheeled in the air, singing in chorus to the rhythm of the wind.

The dragon circled wide, wings cutting across a sky too bright, too perfect.

Carmyra leaned back against him, her voice low, coaxing. "This is where I live, Eldrin. Beyond chains, beyond war. Here, no oaths bind you. No council condemns you. Only joy. Only peace."

She turned her face toward his, hair whipping against his cheek. "You could stay. With me. We could make this ours."

Below, the towers glimmered brighter, as if beckoning. Eldrin's chest ached with longing. He had never seen such beauty — not even in the deepest glades of the Elven Realm. For a moment, he imagined himself descending there, walking its shining halls, free of the weight of prophecy, of bloodlines, of expectation.

Her hand brushed his jaw. "You've carried duty all your life. Haven't you earned this? Haven't you earned me?"

The Aetherstone pulsed once — faint, insistent — but the vision's brilliance dulled it to a shadow.

Eldrin's breath caught, his heart torn between the searing wind of the flight and the warmth of her promise…

Chapter 22

The giants moved like storm clouds through the forest, vast and silent. For all their bulk, their footfalls left no thunder, no crashing trees — only a faint tremor in the soil, a whisper felt more than heard. Their stone-hewn forms bent with the canopy, shifting between trunks as though the Arden itself parted to let them pass.

Behind them, drelves and elves followed, cloaks drawn tight, every step measured to match the uncanny rhythm of their allies. More than once, a younger warrior glanced up, startled at how a shape taller than a watchtower could vanish into the trees and reappear yards ahead. It was not the noise that unnerved them — it was the lack of it.

Lyria kept pace at the front, her mark thrumming hot against her skin. She touched her palm unconsciously, the cut still stinging where blood had sealed the Oath. Chains of blue-green and amber bound them to whatever waited ahead.

Kaelis strode at her side, her eyes scanning the gloom. "I don't like it," she muttered. "How quiet they are. Like ghosts."

"They are not ghosts," Lyria said. "They are titans."

"I'm just glad they are on our side," Kaelis replied, her mouth pressed thin as her eyes flicked skyward. Through the canopy, the clouds gathered as a low rumble threatened a downpour.

"We should be flying. We could be there in half the time."

Lyria shook her head. "Not with dragons above. Or worse — wyverns. The cloaks may not hide us in the open sky."

Reluctantly, Kaelis nodded. The Shadowcloaks blurred well enough in the forest, but in the air, one flare of fear or rage would leave them exposed to every watching eye.

Still, both knew when the moment came, the sky would be theirs again.

The forest was hushed except for the patter of rain. Even the shadows seemed to hold their breath, waiting. No birds chirped, no forest creatures stirred. Only the silence of a forest that remembered old oaths and chose not to interfere.

At last, the lead giant halted, eyes burning as it raised its head to the wind. Its voice rumbled low, as distant thunder muffled by the canopy. "The camp lies in the distance. We smell their smoke."

Through the trees, a faint orange glow flickered — firelight strung in the branches. And beyond that, the outline of cages swaying against the dark.

Eldrin.

Lyria's heart clenched, her wings twitching against the cloak. The mark seared hotter, urgent.

Kaelis caught her arm before she could move. "Wait. We must plan this strike, or we fail it."

But Lyria's breath came sharp, her hand already drifting toward her blade.

The war band halted just beyond sight of the dark elves' camp. Smoke drifted up through the trees, thick with the stench of pitch and charred meat. The faint sound of steel on stone rang from the camp — the Umbrin sharpening blades.

Kaelis crouched low, eyes narrowed. "We need to get closer to watch their movements, to know how many we are up against. Charging in blind is suicide."

Lyria's mark pulsed hot, urging her forward, but even she knew Kaelis was right. "Then we go. You and me," she said, looking at Kaelis.

An elf stepped forward from the band of twenty or so that had joined the drelves. No elf could allow drelves to take all the glory. He was lithe, with fiery eyes and a restless look. His cloak shimmered around him, flickering in and out of sight as though he were half-smoke already. "I will go."

Kaelis studied him.

"I am Erynder. I am the quickest. You drelves have tails that the cloaks don't cover. That might give you away."

A murmur ran through the war-band.

"And I will go with him."

The voice came from a female elf near the back of the war-band. She stepped forward, rain slicking her long red hair, two thin braids framing a pale, steady face. Her emerald eyes shone and were sharp as ice. Her Shadowcloak shimmered without falter, stronger than most, the outline of her form nearly invisible even as she moved.

"I am Seliora," she said, her voice calm, assured. "Two elves see better than one. I can watch his back."

Erynder raised one brow, his ears twitching faintly, but he held his tongue.

Kaelis glanced at Lyria, their eyes meeting in brief understanding. Drelves were hunters, not fools — the Umbrin camp was death wrapped in shadow. A couple of lithe elves would make better spies than the two of them.

Kaelis gave a curt nod. "Two of you, then. No more. Watch for patrols. Count their numbers. When do they change the guard? How many dragons? Mark every detail, every path in and out, and find us a way to release the captives. Do not fight unless attacked. Return with answers — and do not give us away."

The giant leader, Gravorn, bent low, eyes burning through the gloom. His voice rolled like stone on stone. "One step into that firelight, and your shadows will cling to you. Fail, and the enemy will know you long before steel is drawn, and our element of surprise dies with you."

Seliora inclined her head once, unflinching.

Erynder searched her eyes, hunting for the flicker of doubt. Finding none, he gave a sharp nod and pulled his cloak tight. In the next breath, he slipped into the trees, form dissolving into shadow. Seliora followed, her outline vanishing more swiftly than his — swallowed whole by the shadows until nothing remained.

Darkness pooled beneath the cages, heavy and suffocating. Thalendir stirred in restless sleep, sweat slicking his brow. Finnian lay nearby, muttering under his breath as if locked in sleep.

And then — light.

Both elves stood, not in the Arden but in a realm of sky and gold. Clouds blazed around them, pierced by a dragon's vast wings. Upon its back rode Eldrin, whole and strong, his wounds gone, his laughter raw and unguarded as the beast carried him higher.

And he was not alone.

The elf they had both seen earlier — hair like molten gold, eyes blue as sapphires — pressed close against Eldrin.

Thalendir's jaw clenched. His fists curled at his side. Finnian's breath caught, heat rising in his chest.

Her touch lingered on Eldrin's cheek, her smile slow and knowing, as though she *wanted* to be seen. The sight of her beside him sank hooks into both their hearts.

Then the dream shifted. For a heartbeat, Carmyra's gaze flicked toward them, her smile deepening in silent invitation. To Finnian, her eyes lingered with warmth; to Thalendir, they gleamed with recognition.

A green-eyed monster struck like a blade, sharp and merciless, and pierced their souls as the dragon wheeled through the skies, carrying Eldrin and his prize, farther from them. And both elves shared the same hollow ache: the desperate need to claim what Eldrin had.

Then—her voice. A whisper, slipping through the dream.

To Finnian, tenderly: "I will return for you."

To Thalendir, low and knowing: "You are my favorite."

Their breaths caught, the words sinking deep. And as the dragon soared beyond reach, the two elves woke in their cages, hearts pounding with a hunger they could not name…

Chapter 23

Drovane did not stir until the dragons' voices had faded into the hush of the forest. Only then did he slip from the roots, his form melting out of shadow as easily as breath.

Fools.

Zyressa, with her scarred pride. Drakor, all teeth and cunning. Velthar, hungry as a carrion crow. They thought themselves clever, whispering of betrayal as if the Umbrin were deaf. But Drovane had heard every word — and he was no mere servant to be fooled.

He drifted between the trees, steps soundless, the cloak of night clinging close. The Umbrin camp lay ahead, its fires guttering low, towers swaying with the weight of watchers. His kin moved like silhouettes through the branches, their eyes hollow gleams, their whispers rustling like dead leaves. When they noticed him, they stepped aside, bowing heads beneath dark hoods.

When he reached the inner ring, he paused, letting his gaze sweep the cages strung high. The elves hung there still, weak but not broken. And in one of them, the elf being tested, stirred — the golden-haired phantom still twining around his dreams. Drovane's lips curved. Their plan was working. A baited snare. A dangerous game. But if anyone could get the elf to reveal his mark, it would be Camyra.

The dragons' mistake was believing they could steal what belonged to the Umbrin. He'd make sure they didn't live to talk about it.

He moved into the circle of firelight where the other leaders waited — cloaked, their forms shifting like smoke. They inclined their heads as he entered, acknowledging him as one of their own.

"The scaled one's plot treachery," Drovane said, his eyes glinting. "They mean to take the mark for themselves when it awakens. They call us useful — but nothing more. The serpents have no intention of sharing the power of the mark."

A murmur rippled through the circle, sharp as broken glass. The shadows themselves seemed to lean closer, listening.

One of the cloaked figures hissed. "Dragons are liars by nature. Deceivers covered in scales."

Another voice rasped low, old as stone. "And yet… they are useful. Their strength has bought us time. Their fire has cowed the drelves and kept the Arden in fear."

Drovane's lip curled. "Useful like a tool. But all of us discard even the finest tools when their edges become blunted. Do you wish to be the tool, or the hand that wields it?"

The murmurs died. All eyes — gleaming, hollow, unblinking — turned toward him.

Then the Whisper — an unseen voice, thin as smoke, sharp as a blade — rose from the dark.

"Then let them think us blind. Let them think us weak. And when the fire shows itself…" A hiss of laughter coiled through the air. "We will cut their throats in the dark and drink the mark's power for our own."

Shadows swelled, curling around Drovane's shoulders like wings. He inclined his head, satisfaction burning cold behind his eyes.

The dragons thought of themselves as hunters. Soon, they would learn what it meant to be prey.

Seliora pressed herself flat against the tree, breath shallow, the Shadowcloak whispering around her like mist. Firelight and shadow pulsed from the Umbrin camp, and guards shifted, their blades catching sparks as they sharpened them against stone. The air stank of smoke and charred meat.

Erynder crouched nearby, eyes sharp, body taut with restless energy. His cloak flickered faintly as his impatience bled through.

"Hold still," she whispered, barely moving her lips.

His ears twitched, but he obeyed. Together, they watched.

From their vantage point, the camp unfolded in grim detail:

Three cages strung in the branches, the elves swaying within — weak, but alive.

Makeshift watchtowers lashed together, swaying, with Umbrin sentries at every corner.

And worse — the dragons. Three vast shapes coiled in the shadows beyond the fire, their scales glinting in the glow. Even at rest, their eyes burned like furnaces, unblinking.

Erynder's fingers flexed against the bark. "There are more than I thought. Twice the number of sentries. And those beasts…" His gaze flicked toward the dragons. "If they take wing—"

Seliora cut him off with a sharp glance. "Count, don't panic. We came to gather intel, not to carry fear."

He swallowed hard, forcing his eyes back to the task. "Then count with me. I see thirty Umbrin, maybe more. Guard rotations — two at each cage, changed on the hour. And three dragons—" His voice faltered.

Seliora followed his gaze. The scarred green dragon shifted, a low rumble echoing through the camp, while the crooked shape beside her hissed in reply. The third stirred but did not rise, its breath steaming like smoke from the earth itself. Seliora's hand tightened on her sword, every instinct begging her to strike. But she forced her grip steady. Discipline. Patience.

"The dragons will not be our concern if the giants strike true," she said at last. "Mark the paths. Find the weaknesses."

For a long moment, they said nothing, only listened to the whispers of the camp. Then, almost too soft to hear, a sound drifted from the cages — laughter. Faint, delirious, but real. Eldrin's voice carried on the wind.

Seliora's stomach turned cold. "Was that…an elf? Laughing?"

"Aye," said Erynder.

"But…why would a captive laugh?"

Erynder's jaw clenched, eyes narrowing. "He wouldn't. Unless…shadow-magic toys with his mind."

Seliora and Erynder crouched in silence; the camp stretched before them like a nest of embers. The only sounds were the rasp of blades on stone, the hiss of dragon-breath, the slow creak of cages swaying against their ropes.

Then, a shift.

The crooked dragon's head lifted, yellow eyes cutting through the firelight. Its nostrils flared, a low hiss rattling from its throat.

Erynder froze, cloak flickering as his breath hitched.

Seliora pressed her palm against the branch, forcing her cloak tighter, as she mouthed. "Don't move."

The dragon's gaze swept the tree line, lingering where they crouched. For one terrible heartbeat, Seliora felt it see her — as though the Shadowcloak was nothing but thin silk against that ancient stare.

The beast rumbled, wings twitching. A few Umbrin guards looked up, uneasy.

Seliora's hand drifted to her blade.

At last, the crooked dragon snorted and lowered its head again, curling back into the shadows. The guards muttered and returned to their posts.

Only when the hiss of its breath evened did Seliora move, her lips brushing the air. "Now. Go."

Erynder didn't argue. In the next breath, both elves slipped back into the forest, shadows swallowing them whole.

Chapter 24

Buried deep beneath the Drelf Kingdom lay the archives, carved into the mountain's roots and sealed from the living world. Few came here anymore. The stairs wound narrow and steep, their stone worn smooth by centuries of forgotten feet, until they opened into a cavern vast and hollow as a tomb.

Stalactites dripped from the high ceiling, the sound echoing like a clock that measured centuries instead of hours. The air was thick with dust and stone, heavy with the weight of years. Shelves bowed with age lined the walls, laden with scrolls whose ink had long since faded to ghosts.

Nyxari's lamp guttered low, casting long fingers of shadow across the chamber as the archives whispered like a graveyard of words.

She had come seeking knowledge of the second mark, but knowledge here did not rest easily. Some swore the old texts spoke for themselves. Others said a Keeper haunted the place, ink and bone bound to endless duty. She thought it a myth—until the shadows stirred.

The air shivered. From the darkness unfurled a figure half-shaped, its form like ink bleeding through parchment. Its eyes burned faintly blue, hollow as memory.

"You seek what is not yours to find," it rasped.

Nyxari's stood tall, though her hand trembled faintly. The Keeper — it could be no other.

Yet she forced her voice steady. "Not mine to find? Then tell me — whose hands do the scrolls belong to? Yours, or the living?"

The silhouette leaned forward, and the scroll in its grasp pulsed like a heartbeat. "The words are bound to the one who bears the mark. To her, they would open. But to you…"

Nyxari's scales prickled, but she held firm. "I am the one who guards her. The one who raised her, who guides her path. I will stand in her stead."

The figure hissed, the sound like ink sizzling on stone. "Perhaps. But it will cost you."

Her fingers trembled. "Name it."

The Keeper's hollow eyes smoldered, flaring blue in the dark. "A truth for a truth. Give me what you know of the Oath, between drelf and giants. And I will give you what has been forgotten."

Her throat tightened. Every instinct warned her to step back, to leave this cursed place and its bargains behind. But she thought of Lyria — of the chains already wound around her — and forced herself to speak.

"Then take this," Nyxari said at last, her voice sharp though her chest ached. "The mark-bearer has unsealed the Oath from long ago. The giants stand with us to pay their debt. Against the Umbrin… and three dark dragons."

A hiss like parchment tearing filled the cavern. The Keeper convulsed, its form flickering as if the words themselves burned through it. Shadows writhed along the shelves, scrolls trembling on their spines.

"Stone and storm called back to war… giants roused from slumber… dragons entwined with shadow," it rasped, voice cracking like brittle vellum. Its hollow eyes flared bright, searing through Nyxari. "You spend much for a single truth, Veilkeeper. Your heart is bound tightly to the mark bearer."

Nyxari's jaw tightened, though her chest ached with the weight of his words. "Then don't waste what I've given. If my truth is costly, let yours be worth the price."

It leaned closer, shadows stretching long across the shelves. The scroll in its hand pulsed again, brighter, like a heart straining in its last beats.

"Then hear what is written… when the Oath is called, chains shall bind until the next mark emerges."

Her jaw tightened. "You haven't told me anything I did not already know. Who will bear the next mark?"

The Keeper's eyes flickered, its hollow glow deepening as the shadows thickened around it, as parchment-skin, crinkled like dry leaves. "Would you cage fire, Veilkeeper? To name the spark is to snuff it. It lies veiled, hidden among elves. To name it now would unmake it."

Nyxari reached for the scroll. "Tell me! I gave you what I know."

The scroll drifted closer, just out of reach. "Know this: when hearts are tested, the dagger will answer. By fire or by ruin, it will answer."

The figure unraveled, dissolving into smoke and ink. The scroll dropped to the table, brittle edges hissing as if scorched.

Nyxari's hand hovered before she dared touch it. Her scales prickled, her chest tight…*tested? How?* The words rang in her skull like tolling bells.

Her breath quickened. She turned the parchment, scanning the broken lines. The letters blurred, the old magic twisting into vision. Nyxari saw giants striding through fire, their blood mingling with drelves as shadows tore the forest. She saw an elf astride a dragon, laughter on his lips, but his eyes—his eyes were wrong, lit with a light not his own. A golden-haired phantom clung close to him, her smile bright as sunlight yet edged with shadow, her hand pressed to his heart.

Her grip tightened on the brittle scroll until it cracked.

"Eldrin," she whispered, the words barely more than breath. "They will test him… not in strength or valor, but in love."

The lamp flickered once more, shadows leaping across the walls.

Nyxari closed her eyes. She had spoken his name — and speaking it made it real. The battle for the second mark had already begun — and hearts, not blades, would be the first to bleed.

The rain had thinned to a mist, clinging cold to cloaks and armor. Lyria waited at the edge of the war-band, her mark a steady burn at her throat. Every heartbeat seemed to drag against iron chains. They had moved far away from the Umbrin camp, waiting for word from the two spies.

At last, two shadows slipped from the trees. Seliora emerged first, her cloak fading back into shape, red hair damp and plastered to her cheeks. Erynder followed, his chest rising hard, ears flicking as he pulled his hood back.

Kaelis stepped forward sharply. "Well?"

Erynder exhaled, his voice taut. "Worse than we thought. At least thirty Umbrin. Patrols circle the perimeter; guards change on the hour. The captives hang in the center of the camp, surrounded by sentries."

Seliora's eyes cut toward Lyria. "And there are three dragons."

A hush fell over the gathered drelves. Even the giants stilled, eyes narrowing.

"A scarred green one. A crooked runt. And a third — bronze, older, but strong. They do not sleep. Their eyes burn like furnaces, watching everything."

Kaelis swore under her breath. "Three dragons. And thirty Umbrin besides. Charging in would be slaughter."

Erynder bristled, restless. "We must act soon." He shook his head, unsettled. "One captive…was acting strangely. Talking to himself and laughing. As though his mind were not his own."

"Which one?" Lyria's voice was low, edged with dread.

"Eldrin," Seliora said, clipped. "His eyes…they did not belong to him. They burned with something wrong. Something that should not be in an elf."

Lyria's eyes narrowed. "With what?"

Seliora's jaw tightened. "Dark magic."

A chill cut through Lyria. Her mark flared hot, urgent, as though answering some unseen call. Power surged beneath her skin — vast, untested, frightening in its depth. She had felt it before, mingled with Eldrin's, but alone, she did not know its reach. Only that others feared it. Hunted it.

Eldrin.

She clenched her fists, forcing her voice steady. "Then we break the chains. No matter what sorcery binds him."

Gravorn's gaze fixed on her, his rumble low and reverent. "The mark burns brighter than chains or sorcery. We feel its weight, child of blood and storm. Where it leads, we will follow."

The words rolled through the war-band like thunder. The giants bowed their heads, as if acknowledging her place among them.

Kaelis's jaw tightened. She said nothing at first, though her eyes lingered on Lyria — not with doubt in her strength, but with unease at what that strength was becoming. Friend, leader… or something greater? The mark had made her more than drelf, more than kin, and Kaelis's heart warred between pride and fear of losing her to it.

At last, she spoke, her voice low, steady but edged with warning. "We strike like earth, wind, and fire — sudden and unseen. The giants will take on the dragons. We descend from the sky. The others break the guards. And the fire—" her eyes flicked to Lyria, "—that is yours to wield. Just make sure it doesn't consume you."

All eyes turned toward Lyria, as if the decision had already been made — not by her, but by the mark itself. It seared hot on her throat, thrumming like a war drum. She gazed in the direction of the Umbrin camp, imagining Eldrin, Thalendir, and Finnian swaying in the dark. She managed a nod, though in her heart she wondered if their strength — or her mark's — would be enough.

For chains could be broken. But fire, once loosed, could not be called back.

Chapter 25

Wind stung Eldrin's face, cold and sharp, but exhilaration drowned the fear. The dragon's wings carved the sky in thunderous rhythm, each sweep hurling them higher above the world. Below, the forest blurred into a dark sea; rivers flashed silver in the moonlight.

Camyra leaned back against him, her laughter bright as flame. "Do you believe it now?" she called over the wind. "The world could be ours. No chains. No war. Only this."

For a heartbeat, he did believe. The sky belonged to them. The ache of duty, the mark, the weight of his father's voice — all dissolved into wind and light.

Then the dragon tilted, banking toward a valley awash in golden glow. Blossoms of every hue blanketed the hills, their petals glimmering as though brushed with fire. At its heart lay a crystalline pool, reflecting a sun that had no source.

They landed with a grace no dragon of war should have. Camyra slid down and turned, eyes alight, her hand extended. "Come. I want to show you where we belong."

Eldrin followed, boots striking the warm scales. The air smelled of rain and flowers; laughter — his own — seemed to echo faintly through the breeze.

At the water's edge, she stopped. "Look," she whispered. "This is the life you could have. No duty. No burden. No mark to haunt you."

He stared into the pool. His reflection looked back — taller, prouder, a true warrior. Beside him stood Camyra, radiant and sure, her hand resting over his heart.

Then the water trembled. Silver wings shimmered faintly through the reflection, eyes of amethyst looking into his soul.

Lyria.

Guilt cut through him like an arrow. His breath hitched.

Camyra's fingers slid to his jaw, turning him toward her. "Look at me," she murmured, her voice low and commanding. "Only at me."

The air between them thickened. Her scent was honey and smoke, her nearness a storm. When her lips brushed his, the kiss was soft — then deepened, fierce, and consuming. Fire roared through his veins, and for a heartbeat, he wanted nothing but her.

The Aetherstone flared cold against his chest. He gasped, the chill slicing through the warmth like ice in his blood.

Camyra didn't pull away. "You have already chosen," she breathed against his mouth. "All that remains is to let go."

Her eyes glowed with inner fire, wild and blue. "Bond with me, Eldrin. One soul to another. Bound forever."

The word struck him like a blade. Among elves, bonds were sacred — eternal, unbroken even by death. To give one's soul was to surrender utterly.

The Aetherstone pulsed again, hard, freezing the air around them. His heart pounded in two rhythms — her warmth and its warning. The world blurred, edges dissolving into light and shadow.

For a heartbeat, he almost yielded.

Then the Aetherstone struck once more — a pulse like lightning through ice — and the illusion cracked. The valley wavered, blossoms curling to ash, the sky dimming to gray.

Along the forest floor, the mist thickened, curling low, clinging to roots and stone. Every step the giants took toward the Umbrin camp seemed to ripple through the soil, as if the Arden itself braced for what was coming. They loomed like mountains in motion, silent despite their size, their eyes fixed ahead.

Lyria moved at the front of the war-band, her Shadowcloak whispering around her shoulders. But the cloak could not hide the heat of the mark burning at her throat. It thrummed like a drumbeat, louder with every breath, as though it sensed what lay ahead.

She pressed her palm against it, her skin prickling with sparks. For a heartbeat, her vision blurred — not with the campfires ahead, but with dark braids, green eyes, and a voice she could not hear, yet somehow felt. Eldrin.

Her chest tightened. The mark was answering something, pulling her toward it with a ferocity she had never known.

Kaelis fell into step beside her, eyes sharp, sword balanced against her shoulder. "The giants are ready. So are my warriors. But you—" her gaze flicked to the glow beneath Lyria's cloak, "—you burn hotter with every minute. What's wrong"?

The mark seared against Lyria's skin. For one fleeting instant, the world tilted, firelight flooding her sight though no torches burned nearby. She saw Eldrin astride a dragon, golden hair brushing his cheek, blue eyes fixed only on him. The she-elf's smile was radiant; her hand pressed to his heart, her lips pressed to his, as though he already belonged to her.

Lyria staggered, breath catching. Jealousy, sharp and raw, pierced her like a blade. She had told herself she could not be with him — mark or no mark — but seeing him with her, cut deeper than she could bear.

The vision shattered, leaving only the burn of her mark and a hollow ache beneath her ribs. The world came rushing back

— the hiss of wind, the scent of smoke — but none of it felt real.

She forced her voice steady. "He's falling…"

Kaelis's head whipped toward her, eyes narrowing. "What? Who's falling?"

Lyria hesitated, her pulse still racing. The vision seared behind her eyelids — Eldrin's face, his laugh, the touch of his hand… their power joined — and then *her*: the golden-haired beauty beside him, smiling as though she owned his heart. The ache clawed at Lyria's chest, stealing her breath.

When she finally spoke, her voice was barely a whisper. "Eldrin. He's falling for her."

Kaelis caught her arm, yanking her to a halt. Her sword dipped low, the point biting into the earth. "Falling for who? Tell me what you saw."

Lyria shook her head. "It was only a glimpse. Firelight. An… elf. Beautiful." The words came bitter. "She had him — smiling, laughing —her lips on his. As though the world belonged to her."

Kaelis's eyes hardened, not with doubt, but with fury. "Then it's a snare. A trick of the Umbrin, or worse. You cannot falter now. If your mark burns, it's because he's in danger. Remember that."

Lyria's mark throbbed, as if answering Kaelis's warning. She nodded once, but the ache in her chest lingered — sharper now, tangled in a jealousy she could neither name nor banish.

"We strike at dawn," Kaelis said, releasing her arm. Her voice was cold iron. "And if this phantom tries to keep him, we'll cut her from him — one way or another."

Lyria pulled her cloak tighter, though the heat of the mark burned through, a beacon that refused to be hidden. Her heart whispered his name — *Eldrin* — and the sound of it startled her, even now.

Gravorn bent low as he walked, eyes searing the mist. His voice rumbled like mountains grinding together. "The camp lies ahead. When you give the signal, we strike as storm and shadow. My kin will take the dragons. You and yours handle the rest."

The elves shifted nearby — Erynder with his blade half-drawn, Seliora murmuring a quiet incantation that shimmered faintly in the air. Their faces were pale beneath the shroud of fog, but their eyes burned with the same fire as the drelves beside them. Old grudges meant nothing now; only survival remained.

The drelves tightened their formation, wings twitching beneath their cloaks, the sky calling to them like blood to a wound. The elves adjusted their grip on spear and bow, each waiting for the same unspoken signal.

Lyria's breath caught, sharp as a blade. Whatever held Eldrin in its snare — she could not, would not let it claim him. Not without one hell of a fight.

She lifted her chin, her voice cutting through mist and silence alike, carrying to every ear that followed her.

"At dawn," she said, steady as fire, "we break the chains."

Chapter 26

Four riders moved through the Enchanted Forest, beneath a pale moon. It's light falling silver through the canopy. The riders rode single-file, following the old patrol paths that wound northward from the Elven citadel.

Aldareth led with the quiet authority of a warrior who had seen more battles than most elves would ever live through. His horse, a dark gelding, was sure-footed and steady, its hooves barely whispering against the moss. A sword rode at his hip, his hand resting near the hilt — not from nerves, but habit. His presence alone steadied the others; he was the Master Trainer, after all — the one who had taught half the kingdom's warriors how to hold a blade.

Caelith followed close, eyes sharp, his dapple-grey mare keeping perfect step with Aldareth's mount. Aelar rode behind, broad-shouldered and calm, a silent pillar even when the night pressed close. Aerion brought up the rear, her bow half drawn, her gaze sweeping every shadow and every bough above them.

The forest seemed to hush around their passing — only the rhythmic thrum of hooves and the soft creak of leather broke the stillness. The scent of pine and damp earth filled the air, mingling with the faint shimmer of moonlit mist.

Yet even here, beneath the boughs of their own realm — the Enchanted Forest, warded by generations of Elven blood — unease lingered. No birds stirred. No wind touched the leaves. No crickets sang.

They crossed streams swollen by recent rains, their mounts splashing through cold water that caught moonlight in silver ribbons. The king had sent some of his finest steeds for the spies, and the elves were grateful for their strength and endurance. Twice, they followed narrow deer trails that curved north toward the mountains, winding between the roots of ancient oaks.

By midnight, the forest paths had tightened, the soft moss giving way to rougher ground. Roots knotted the earth beneath their mounts, slowing their pace. Mist thickened as they climbed, cold clinging to their cloaks and hair. Every sound seemed sharper — the creak of a branch, the snap of a twig, the distant rush of unseen water.

It was there at the river ford that the first unease fell upon them. Aerion reined in her mare, the animal's ears flicking back, nostrils flaring. Her hand rose in warning. The others halted, hooves stamping softly in the shallows, steam rising where warm breath met cold air.

"Something follows," Aerion murmured.

The water lapped at the stones, its rhythm steady—too steady. Even the horses seemed to listen, muscles coiled tight beneath saddle and leather. Mist drifted low across the ford, curling around fetlocks and hooves like grasping fingers.

Across the opposite bank, two red embers flared in the gloom. Then another pair. And another.

Caelith swore under his breath, blade sliding free. Aelar's grip tightened on his sword. "Eyes. Dozens of them."

Aldareth's jaw set, his voice low and sure. "They don't belong to any beast born of this forest."

The air changed—dense, metallic. Then came the sound: the slow grind of clawed hooves dragging through mud, the hiss of breath that reeked of scorched iron.

The mist broke apart as something vast moved within it—shapes hulking and misshapen, half-shrouded in smoke. A rank stench rolled across the ford.

Nemods.

Their mounts—the nightmarish Shadowmanes—emerged first, horse-shaped only in mockery. Their hides gleamed like wet obsidian, stretched thin over bone, clawed hooves carving deep gouges into the stones. Upon their backs, the nemods crouched low, wolf-like heads tilting as ember-filled eyes fixed on the elves.

"They're still here—on our land?" Aerion breathed, nocking an arrow. "I thought we'd driven this rot from our borders."

"Apparently not," Aldareth said grimly.

The lead nemod raised its head and released a sound between a growl and a scream—a signal. The others answered in unison. The air itself seemed to warp as they charged, talons slamming into the shallows, steam rising where molten veins met the river's chill.

"Form up!" Aldareth barked.

Caelith's mare reared, hooves lashing as a Shadowmane lunged from the mist. His sword came down in a bright arc, striking the rider's arm. The blow split black stone and sinew, molten light spraying like sparks from a forge—but the creature did not fall. It howled, twisting its head to bite.

Aerion's arrow flew, piercing the joint of its neck. The nemod convulsed, snarling, before toppling from its mount—its body already burning away into smoke and cinder.

Aelar wheeled his stallion to flank her, shield raised as another nemod swept low. Its claws screeched against the steel, carving trails of heat across the metal. He gritted his teeth, shoving it back, the scent of burning leather choking the air.

"They're trying to drive us from our own forest!" Aerion shouted.

"Not today!" Aldareth roared. His sword flashed again, clean and brutal. The blade met a Shadowmane's neck; black ichor erupted, sizzling against his arm. The beast shrieked and stumbled, collapsing into the current where the water hissed and boiled.

The elves pressed tighter, horses stamping in fear as the nemods circled. Red eyes ringed the fog.

Caelith's voice rasped. "There are too many."

"Hold!" Aldareth snapped. "They hunt, not swarm. They're testing our strength."

Another scream tore through the haze—one of rage, not pain. The remaining nemods began to close in, their bodies flickering like shadows bound by flame.

Then the ground trembled.

The river beside them surged high, water flashing silver with ancient magic. It crashed across the ford in a sudden wave, sweeping several nemods away. Roots writhed from the riverbank, snaring Shadowmanes mid-leap, crushing their limbs until the light died from their eyes.

Aldareth looked toward the forest, his gaze sharp. "The forest defends itself."

Aerion lowered her bow, breath shaking. "It knows they don't belong here."

The last nemod hissed—a sound like hatred given voice—before its body began to unravel. Smoke poured from its wounds as it and its mount dissolved into ash.

Silence followed. Only the hiss of cooling water and the whisper of trees.

Aldareth sheathed his sword. "The darkness still seeps into our land," he said.

Caelith exhaled, glancing toward the misted horizon. "Then we'd best stop it."

Aerion looked back over her shoulder, unease still sharp in her eyes. "If such creatures prowl this close to the citadel… what waits for us deeper north?"

Caelith reined his gelding closer, sheathing his sword with a snap. "Nothing we can't cut down." His words were brave, but the tightness in his jaw betrayed him.

Aldareth's gaze lingered on the mist beyond the ford. He sheathed his blade, slow and deliberate. "Pray there are no more on the road ahead," he said at last. "If there are… our forest will not be there to help next time."

No one spoke after that. They crossed the river in silence, hooves breaking the mirror surface, the water cold as iron against their boots. Ahead, the path vanished into fog — leading them toward the mountains, and the darkness that waited beyond.

Three cages swayed above the Umbrin camp, chains groaning as the captives shifted restlessly. The night air crackled with firelight, its smoke stinging eyes and lungs.

Below, cloaked figures stood over a pile of confiscated steel. Blades glimmered faintly in the firelight — swords, knives, even bows stripped of their quivers.

One of the dark elves reached down, fingers curling around a dagger unlike the others. Its hilt gleamed faintly, runes etched into the steel as though they breathed with their own light. Eldrin's dagger.

From his cage, Eldrin tensed, his breath catching in his chest.

The Umbrin warrior lifted it high, sneering. "What's this? A trinket dressed as steel?"

Another Umbrin leaned close, his eyes narrowing. "Careful. There is power on that blade."

"Power?" The first scoffed. "All power bows to shadow." He wrapped his hand fully around the hilt.

The dagger flared. A searing white fire burst across the blade, devouring shadow as if it drank it. The Umbrin shrieked, dropping it at once. His hand smoked, flesh seared black where he had touched it.

Above, Thalendir's eyes widened. Finnian gripped the bars of his cage, voice low. "Bloody elves… what's in that dagger?"

Eldrin could not tear his eyes from the blade. It lay in the dirt, pulsing faintly as if alive. The Aetherstone warmed at his side, answering the fire. His mother's dagger. His blood's dagger.

The scorched Umbrin staggered back, cradling his ruined hand. His fellows recoiled, whispering like dry leaves. None dared reach for the dagger again.

Thalendir's voice rasped through the dark, half disbelief, half awe. "That blade belongs to you, brother."

Eldrin strained forward, every fiber of him reaching for it though it lay far below. The fire dimmed, waiting — as if it too longed for his hand.

But he could not touch it.

Something moved beneath the cages. The shadows thickened — not as smoke, but as substance, rippling as water disturbed. A chill swept through the camp, and the fire flickered low, bowing to the dark.

Then she stepped through it.

Camyra.

She emerged from the trembling veil of shadow, the flicker of flame bending around her form. Her hair caught the light like molten glass, her face serene — too serene — her eyes deep as midnight.

Finnian's breath caught. "She's real," he whispered. "She's bloody real."

Thalendir muttered, eyes narrowing. "Dream and flesh both — how is that possible?"

Camyra's voice answered them, soft and cold. "Because your wards have thinned. The veil between what is and what waits has grown weak. The dagger did that — its light calls me, as his blood does."

Her gaze lifted, finding Eldrin through the bars.

He froze. The Aetherstone on his belt throbbed once, faint but insistent.

"Tell me…" Camyra's voice cut through the murmurs. "What happened?"

The Umbrin who still clutched his blackened hand sneered through his pain. "We took the knife from him earlier," he spat, nodding toward Eldrin. "But it did not burn until now."

Camyra's smile curved slowly and knowingly. "Of course not."

She stepped closer, the firelight bending away from her as she passed. "Because it does not burn *for* him." Her eyes gleamed as they met Eldrin's. "It burns *with* him. The mark is calling."

A hush rippled through the camp. All eyes turned to the dagger where it lay in the dirt, its glow quickening, fire seething along the edge as though it breathed in rhythm with her steps.

Her gaze lifted to the cages. Eldrin met her eyes, and in that instant the Aetherstone at his side throbbed — cold, insistent — while the dagger flared brighter, defiant, alive.

Finnian's grip tightened on the bars, breath sharp. "She seeks Eldrin's power," he muttered, low enough only Thalendir might hear.

Thalendir said nothing, but his jaw worked, his hazel eyes locked on her. The mark, the dagger, Eldrin — all pieces of a puzzle. And now, this irresistible female…

The dagger pulsed in answer, white fire arcing along its edge — not welcoming, but warning. The dark elves stepped back, murmuring uneasily, their whispers rustling. Yet no one dared reach for the weapon again.

Above, Eldrin's breath caught. The dagger's fire called to him as surely as Camyra's gaze — two forces pulling, one of blood and one of shadow.

And somewhere deep inside, the Aetherstone beat harder, colder, as though it alone knew what was coming.

Her hand hovered just above the hilt — not touching, only testing — daring the light to defy her. The dagger's glow quickened, flaring white-hot where her fingers lingered above it, sparks rippling through the air.

Camyra's lips curved, faint and knowing. "Ah… so the blade resists. And perhaps the elf does as well."

Eldrin's chest tightened. Between the dagger's radiance and her unblinking gaze, he could not tell which would consume him first.

Chapter 27

Shadows pressed thick between the trees as the Umbrin's fires burned low, whispering, listening. Drovane stood at the edge of the circle, the dagger's flare still etched behind his eyes like lightning after a storm. The others muttered, restless, their cloaks shifting like smoke.

"They will come," he said at last, his voice low and sharp. "The drelves, the elves, perhaps even more. They will attack soon. And yet, we still don't know which one is the mark bearer."

A murmur rippled through the ring, but in the silence that followed, another voice slithered through the dark — thin as a blade, soft as ash.

The Whisper.

"Let them come. Chains rattle loudest just before they break. And when the mark shows itself…and it will…" A hiss of laughter coiled around them.

Drovane bowed his head, though his lips curved faintly. "But how do we get the mark to appear?"

"We do not summon fire, Drovane. When a spark strikes, fire burns. She will strike it soon enough. And when it blazes…" the laughter thinned to a hiss, "…we will claim it — elf, dagger, mark-all — swallowed by shadow."

Beyond the firelight, three vast shapes crouched low among the trees.

Zyressa's scarred hide shimmered faintly as she raised her head, smoke curling from her jaws. "The Umbrin plot," she growled. "Do you hear their whispers? They mean to take the mark for themselves."

Velthar's bronze tail lashed, gouging furrows in the earth. His wings rattled with a sound like old armor. "Let them try. Their shadows burn as quickly as leaves in fire."

Drakor slithered closer, his crooked wings twitching, eyes gleaming with sly hunger. "Do not be blind. The dark elves are not our only concern. Others will come. Drelves. Elves. Fools who believe they can defeat us." He leaned forward, teeth glinting. "When shadow and flame clash, that is when we strike. While they bleed each other dry, we take what is ours — the blade, the elf, the fire in his blood."

Zyressa's smoke deepened, her voice low, edged with scorn. "If the blade allows it. You saw what it did to the Umbrin's hand. It remembers its master. And it may not choose you."

Drakor's grin widened, jagged and cruel. "Then I will make it bow to a new master. When the Elf is dead, the dagger, the mark, and its power will be ours."

Velthar said nothing, but his eyes glowed, watching the others like a carrion crow circling the dying.

The three crouched in silence, their eyes burning like furnaces through the night. But it was not trust that bound them — only ambition. Each imagined the mark's power was theirs, and theirs alone.

The rescue would come. The battle would rage. But in the end, it was not the Drelves or the Umbrin who would claim the prize.

It would be the dragons.

The mist was a living thing, pooling in hollows, clinging to cloaks and boots. Lyria's senses sharpened with every step—the mark burning like a drum at her throat, Kaelis at her elbow, giants a slow shadow behind. The forest seemed to inhale and hold itself, listening.

Something moved aside from the trunks—not the soft slip of an elf, but a quick, nervous scuttle that did not belong to any creature they hunted. A flash of legs, a glint of green, and a small shape dropped from the underbrush and darted along the roots.

Lyria's hand went to her blade without thinking. "Spy," she breathed.

Kaelis was already gone, a lean arrow of motion as she sprinted after it. The rest of the war-band tightened in behind, silent as sap on a bough. Even the giants shifted, eyes narrowing as if favoring a particular trunk with their gaze.

The skitterling was clever and frightened—its mosaic feathers were shivering, legs a blur. It ran as if it had blood on its heels, weaving under roots and over deadfall. Seliora slipped between two trunks and cut it off; Erynder darted forward and blocked its path. There was no honor in hunting such things—no glory—but the elves were hunters all the same.

Kaelis stooped, swift as a hawk, and snatched the creature by the back before it could twist away. It shrieked—a thousand thin, metallic notes—and its legs beat the air. Up close, its eyes were yellow mirrors, frantic and stupid with fear.

"Who sent you?" Kaelis demanded, voice low enough for only the skitterling to hear. Its mandibles clicked; it replied in a hissing tongue that made the drelves' teeth ache.

The creature thrashed in Kaelis's grip, its wings snapping open with a dry crackle. It beat at the air, dragging them both a step sideways before she braced it against a trunk. Its eyes—round, dark, yet impossibly soft—blinked up at her, wet with a glimmer that almost looked like pleading.

Lyria's mark burned hotter, her hand twitching toward her blade. "It knows too much already. Kill it."

The skitterling keened, high and thin, a sound halfway between a child's cry and metal scraping. Its legs curled close to its body, and its eyes widened, shimmering with fear.

Seliora tilted her head, watching. "Look at it. It begs."

Kaelis's lip curled. "Don't be fooled. Spies are born to beg. That's their only weapon."

Still, she hesitated. The creature's words came again—broken clicks, half-hisses. Scaled… crooked… dragon. Its gaze flicked between them all, as if offering the truth itself as ransom for its life.

Erynder stepped forward. "It must not return to them." He pulled a leather travel sack from his belt, its mouth wide and dark. Kaelis shoved the skitterling inside. The creature twisted, scraping its wings against the cloth, and then it went still. Its eyes caught theirs one last time before Kaelis tied the bag shut.

The war-band stood in uneasy silence.

Gravorn bent low, eyes narrowing on the sack. His voice rumbled like a stone dragged through the earth. "Spies travel fast. They do not return empty. If it has not returned, the sender may already see through its eyes… or wonder why its vision has gone dark." His teeth ground audibly.

A ripple of unease spread through the band.

Kaelis tightened the knot, her jaw set. "Then we move before they discover it missing."

Lyria's hand still hovered near her blade. The mark pulsed hard, furious, as if demanding the spy's death. But the memory of its pleading eyes gnawed at her. If it had more to tell—more about Eldrin, about the dragons—perhaps it was worth keeping alive for now.

"Keep it," she said at last. Her voice was low, steady. "But guard it well. Perhaps we can use the little informer to our advantage."

Kaelis nodded once, though her eyes still burned with distrust. She slung the bag across her back. Inside, the creature shifted faintly, its wings rustling. Then, just as they turned to go, the sack gave one soft, deliberate twitch—like a heartbeat. And then it stilled.

The war-band moved on, but the mist seemed heavier now, as though the forest itself knew they carried more than their own secrets. They melted into the dark, boots and claws and stone moving as one. Behind them, the wind whispered. Ahead, the camp burned on, unaware that its watchers were being watched—and that the war had stepped up a beat.

Chapter 28

Veiled by thin clouds, the sun rose with its muted light, spilling warmth across the land. The band of four moved north along forgotten trails, their horses' hooves thudding softly against moss and loam.

Aldareth led, astride his gelding, his posture straight, the quiet authority of a commander etched into every movement. Caelith followed close, his horse's breath steaming in the morning chill, his eyes never still as they swept the horizon. Aelar's stallion carried him with steady patience, and Aerion brought up the rear, her bow always half-drawn, ears flicking to every rustle in the brush.

The deeper they pressed into the wilds, the heavier the silence grew. No wind stirred the leaves. No birds called. Even the rivers whispered faintly, as though fearful of being heard. The horses' breaths sounded loud in the hush, their flanks damp with sweat despite the cold.

By dusk's edge, they reached the ridges. Mist pooled thick in the hollows below — a vast white sea stretching beneath them. From its depths, bones jutted like broken teeth, ribs the size of towers, skulls split and blackened by ancient fire.

The Dragon Graveyard.

The riders halted, breath misting in the chill air. Even the horses stilled, ears flat, nostrils flaring as if scenting ghosts. The weight of the place pressed down on them all — heavy, old, sacred in its ruin. None spoke. The air itself seemed to hold its breath over that cursed ground.

"Keep moving," Aldareth said at last, his voice low but firm. "The dead do not sleep easily. We ride light and do not linger."

They obeyed without a word. Hooves struck stone, iron shoes echoing faintly as they followed the ridge path. Even Caelith's usual fire dimmed, his jaw tight against the urge to speak. Aerion's bow hand trembled once, though her arrow never wavered.

The mist shifted. An icy wind curled up from below, carrying with it the faintest scent of ash. Aerion's sharp eyes caught movement — a flicker of scales deep among the bones — but when she blinked, it was gone.

Her mare sidestepped nervously, breath pluming in short bursts. "Something moves down there," she murmured.

Aldareth's hand dropped to his sword, knuckles pale against the hilt. "Then we move faster."

They pressed on, the path narrowing into a jagged trail. The horses' hooves clattered against rock, sending small stones tumbling into the mist. Far below, the graveyard slept — or waited.

At last, the ridges gave way to broken ground that sloped toward the mountains. It was there, where the land folded into shadow, that they felt it — the first stirring of another presence.

Not an enemy. Not beast. Something older.

The air itself seemed to whisper, carrying words too faint to understand. The horses tossed their heads, uneasy, hooves shifting restlessly on the stones. A chill ran down each rider's spine.

A hush fell over them all.

Even Aldareth's hand shifted toward his sword.

From the gloom ahead, a shape detached from the stone, cloaked in shadow that caught what little light remained. Her eyes burned bright, knowing and unblinking.

"You tread far from your kingdom," she said, her voice low, resonant, threaded with the weight of visions. "And closer to truths you may not wish to find."

The figure's gaze swept over each of them, as though weighing their worth. The mist coiled tighter around her, reluctant to let her go.

Aldareth's grip tightened on his sword hilt. His voice cut through the hush. "Who are you?"

The shape stepped forward, and the shadows bled back. Her silver-streaked hair caught the faintest light, and the obsidian charms in her braids glinted like stars. Violet eyes fixed on them, sharp and unblinking, as though they pierced beyond flesh into thought itself. Scaled markings shimmered faintly along her arms, the glow of old magic threading just beneath her skin.

"I am Nyxari," she said, her voice low and resonant, heavy with memory. "Veilkeeper of the drelves. Guardian of what should remain hidden… and what must be revealed."

The horses shifted, snorting, as if they too felt the pressure of her gaze. The four elves exchanged glances, tension knotting between them. Aerion's bow dipped slightly, though her eyes stayed wary. Caelith muttered a curse under his breath, fire flashing in his restless stare. Aelar's steady calm faltered for the first time, his hand brushing the knife at his hip.

Nyxari's gaze lingered on Aldareth last, unblinking, searching. "You seek the mark-bearer. And your prince. But you do not yet grasp the weight of what you chase. Prophecy does not open its path to blades and oaths alone. It demands more."

It was Aldareth who answered, his voice calm but iron-edged. "We were sent. By Gantar, the sage of our people. He felt it — through the Aetherstone. Eldrin is in danger."

Her gaze sharpened, faint light flickering in the scaled markings along her arms. "Danger…" she echoed, the word tasting bitter on her tongue. "Yes. Not by blade, nor by flame. But by shadows spun fine as silk. A snare draped in beauty. Gantar felt it too, didn't he?"

Caelith bristled, his jaw tight. "We were told Eldrin was ensnared. But not by what?"

Nyxari tilted her head, as though listening to whispers only she could hear. The charms in her braids clicked faintly. "Not by *what*. By *who*. A mask of gold, a voice sweet as honey. She wears the likeness of an elf, but she is not of your kind. Already she coils around him, and the mark trembles for it."

The elves stiffened. Aerion's bow hand trembled, though her aim never wavered. "Then we are already too late."

"No," Nyxari said, her tone suddenly sharp, cutting through their doubt like steel. "Not too late." Her gaze bore into Aldareth. "But, you must move swiftly, and not only with swords. Shadows cannot be cut. They must be unmasked. If you would rescue Eldrin, you must see past what he sees — or you will lose him before the battle even begins."

The silence that followed was heavy, all four elves absorbing the weight of her words.

"Gantar was right," she murmured at last. "The prince is caught in a snare — spun of beauty, shadow, and desire. Swords will not break it. Only one thing can."

Her hand brushed the scaled markings on her arm, the faint shimmer of light rippling across them as though remembering what her voice could not.

"The dagger he carries. Born of fire, tempered by oath. When the time comes, he must strike with it — or be lost forever."

The words sank into silence, sharp as any blade.

Caelith swallowed, his hand flexing near his sword. "Then we must reach him. Before it's too late."

Nyxari's expression softened, though her eyes burned with urgency. "Yes. Carry that truth to him. Remind him of what he holds. Without the dagger, no strength, no mark, no bond will save him."

Her voice faded into the dark as she stepped back. The mountain mist swallowed her form until only her violet gaze lingered like twin stars. Then even that was gone, leaving the elves and their mounts alone with the weight of prophecy.

The firelight bent strangely in the Umbrin camp, shadows licking higher whenever Camyra moved. She stood below the cages, her hair catching every flicker, her face beautiful and terrible all at once.

Eldrin leaned against the bars, his hands gripping the bone. His pulse raced — the Aetherstone throbbed cold at his side, yet her nearness burned hotter than any forge.

"You feel it, don't you?" Camyra's voice was soft, but it carried, winding through the camp like smoke. "The freedom I offer. No council. No chains. No blood that weighs on you. Only me."

She lifted her eyes, locking onto his. "All it takes is a vow. Speak it, Eldrin. Promise yourself to me, here, before all who doubt you. Let the world see who you choose."

The words struck like arrows.

From the cage above, Thalendir's fists curled white around the bars, his jaw hard enough to crack stone. "Don't you dare," he hissed, though Eldrin could not be sure if it was to Camyra — or to himself.

Finnian shifted, his breath sharp, muttering low. "Eldrin… don't. She means to take your power." He cut himself off, biting hard against the swell of anger twisting through him.

Camyra turned her gaze upward, catching them both with a smile that gleamed like a blade.

"Do you hear?" she purred. "They burn with envy because they know what you already know — that you were never theirs to keep."

Her voice softened, velvet over steel. "Say the words, Eldrin. One vow, and I am yours. Forever."

The Aetherstone flared against his ribs — cold, urgent, alive.

Her hand rose, fingers brushing the air between them as though she could reach through the bars. "Choose me," she whispered. "Now. Before them all."

The air thickened, charged with her will. It pressed against him, a storm made of silk and shadow. Eldrin's pulse hammered. His breath came shallow. For a moment — one perilous heartbeat — her beauty filled the world, drowning thought and reason alike.

No.

His fingers closed around the Aetherstone beneath his tunic. Frost spread through his palm, cutting through the haze. The mark's echo pulsed faintly in his chest — Lyria's light, distant but still there. Still his.

Camyra's smile faltered. "You fight it," she said softly. "How noble." Her voice dropped, a hiss wrapped in honey. "And how useless."

The dagger blazed below, white fire erupting along its blade. The light struck her face, and for an instant, the illusion cracked — her beauty warping at the edges, something serpentine flickering beneath the skin.

Eldrin staggered back, forcing the words through clenched teeth. "I'll never be yours."

Camyra's expression smoothed again, the crack vanishing as swiftly as it came. Her lips curved, calm, certain. "Not yet," she whispered. "But you will."

The mist thickened, curling like smoke around the war-band as they moved. Each step seemed heavier than the last, dragging against Lyria's chest. Her mark burned—not steady, but restless, pulsing in uneven rhythm.

At first, it was bearable.

Then it wasn't.

A cry tore from her lips before she could stop it. She doubled over, clutching at her throat as the Shadowcloak slipped from her shoulders. Silver fire blazed along her skin, alive and furious, as if the mark itself wanted to tear free.

Kaelis was at her side in an instant, gripping her arm. "Lyria—what is it?"

Lyria's vision fractured. For an instant, she saw firelight, saw Eldrin's face lit in gold, his hand clutching the Aetherstone, his jaw set in defiance. And beside him—her. The golden-haired elf, palm splayed across his chest, whispering words Lyria couldn't hear.

The image snapped apart. The pain stayed.

"He's resisting," Lyria gasped, voice raw. "But her power… It's binding him. I can feel it."

The giants slowed, their steps rumbling like distant thunder. Gravorn bent low, ember eyes narrowing, the heat of his breath curling through the mist. "The bond pulls at the light," he rumbled. "If it seals, shadow claims him."

From the Skitterling's satchel came a sudden rustle—violent, urgent. Its shrill cry split the air, a sound that made even the giants flinch.

Kaelis tightened her hold, her own Shadowcloak rippling as if alive. "Don't let it take him. Use it, Lyria—bend the mark before it bends you."

Lyria gritted her teeth, forcing her focus through the pain. The mark's light flickered, wild and unsteady, wavering between brilliance and shadow. She reached inward—toward the bond that tied them across distance and fate.

"Eldrin," she whispered, her breath trembling. "Hold on. I'm coming."

The mark flared hotter, a living brand beneath her skin. Her wings twitched beneath the cloak, aching for release. The air shimmered, heat distorting the mist—then, through the haze above, something vast moved.

A shadow of light.

A shape too immense to belong to earth.

Wings spread wide, white as starlight, gliding silently over the canopy before dissolving into cloud. Yet in her heart, she knew.

Seralyth.

The white dragon had come before—in visions, in dreams—but this was no dream. The air hummed with her presence, ancient and pure.

The mark's fire eased, its fury tempered to a steady glow. A whisper touched her mind, soft as wind through snow:

Move swiftly, child of storm… before the bond is sealed.

Lyria's breath steadied. "He's not lost," she said aloud, her voice stronger now. "Not yet. But we must hurry."

The last tremor of pain left her limbs. Her wings unfurled slightly, catching the silvered light. She turned to Kaelis, to Gravorn, to every waiting face.

Her voice cut through the mist like steel drawn in silence. "Ready yourselves," she commanded. "We strike. No more waiting."

The mist stirred—alive, electric—as the war-band shifted around her. Above, the clouds rolled, pale and restless, as if the heavens themselves had heard.

Chapter 29

The Drelves stirred, wings twitching beneath their cloaks. Kaelis's weapon gleamed faintly in the dim light, her eyes fierce but wary. Even Seliora and Erynder, shadows themselves, shifted with restless energy.

But it was Gravorn who moved. The giant bent low, his eyes burning like coals banked too long. When he spoke, the ground seemed to hum with it.

"You speak as flame, child of storm. But fire alone will not carry us into that camp. The Umbrin weave shadows deep, and dragons coil above their lair. To strike is one thing… to return is another."

Lyria met his gaze, her mark thrumming hot at her throat. "Then tell me, Gravorn. How do we return?"

A silence settled, thicker than the mist. The other giants shifted, unease creaking through their massive frames. At last, Gravorn straightened, his voice like stone grinding on stone.

"There is one who might open the way. One older than my kind, older than your blood. But his roots do not stir lightly."

Kaelis frowned. "Who?"

"The Tree Sage," Gravorn rumbled, bowing his head as if naming him was an act of reverence. "He sleeps deep beneath the Arden, bound to its heart. We have not called him since the Oath was first sworn." His gaze swept them all, heavy with warning. "And to wake him is to wake the forest itself. He does not answer without cost."

The Drelves exchanged uneasy glances, the air between them tightening like a drawn bowstring. Seliora's mouth pressed thin, her shadow cloak whispering against itself, as though even the fabric recoiled.

"What cost?" Lyria asked.

Gravorn's ember eyes burned low. "The painful kind," he rumbled. "He may ask for blood… or a vow you cannot break. Perhaps worse — a piece of what you are."

A silence followed, heavy and close.

"But he alone can unbind the roots that strangle that camp," Gravorn went on, voice deep as thunder through stone, "and open the tunnels below. Paths for your warriors to strike unseen — and to escape, should the tide turn against you."

He looked toward the distant ridge, where the Umbrin fires glimmered faintly through the mist. "Without him," Gravorn said, "we strike… and die in the same breath."

Lyria's chest rose and fell, the weight of his words pressing hard against her ribs. The mark at her throat pulsed, hot and relentless, as though it too agreed.

Around her, the others stood tense and silent — Seliora's jaw tight, the younger scouts' eyes wide as their ears twitched. Even the giants had stilled, their faces grim and waiting. So many lives, all looking to her.

Impatience flared like a spark in her chest. They couldn't afford more delay. Every heartbeat wasted was risky for the captives. For Eldrin.

She lifted her chin, the mark burning brighter against her skin. "Then summon him," she said, voice steady though her pulse thundered in her ears. "Whatever the cost — we face it."

The ground itself seemed to listen. A faint tremor rippled beneath their feet, as if the roots already knew what was coming. The air thickened — not with fear, but with expectation.

Gravorn lowered to one knee, pressing a massive hand into the soil. His eyes dimmed, and for the first time, his voice lost its edge of stone and became something older, heavier.

The other giants followed suit, their vast palms sinking into the earth. A tremor rippled outward, subtle at first, then rolling deep beneath their feet.

From its shoulders, and its face was a hollowed knot, eyes glowing faintly green.

None dared speak. Even the giants fell silent, watching as bark split and roots coiled The Tree Sage.

Its voice was like wind through dead branches. "Blood of storm. Child of oath. You call me for a path through shadow?"

Lyria stepped forward, though her mark burned hot in warning. "I do."

For a moment, the forest grew quiet — mist curling closer, roots whispering beneath the soil. Then the voice came again, older, heavier. "The forest requires balance. Everything has a cost."

Lyria didn't hesitate. Her pulse thundered, but her words were steady. "Name it. Whatever it is, I will pay."

The Sage tilted its head, bark creaking. "I require something that will not return."

Kaelis shifted sharply beside her. "Her life is not yours to claim."

"No," the Sage said, roots writhing at its feet. "Not her life. A memory… of someone. The forest will drink it, and the way will open."

Lyria's heart hammered. A memory? She thought of her mother's face, of Kaelis's hand clasped in hers when they were girls, of Seralyth's voice whispering in dreams. Which would it take?

Kaelis seized her wrist. "Don't. You don't know what it will take from you."

"I don't need to know," Lyria said, her voice low, steady despite the ache in her throat. "If it leads to Eldrin's freedom, to breaking the chains, then I must let it go."

The Sage's gaze burned into her. "I will pick. Once chosen, you cannot change your mind. Do you give it freely?"

Lyria hesitated only a breath before she whispered, "Yes."

The Tree Sage's roots surged, curling tight around her ankles, bark biting like cold iron. Its hollow voice pressed into her mind.

"The forest will feed on the memories taken… and what it drinks, it never returns."

The mark seared, dragging, resisting. It was futile.

Lyria's vision fractured — then reformed.

She was back in the Enchanted Forest, wounded and trembling. Then, Eldrin's arms steadied around her as he dragged her toward Gantar's cottage. She was in pain, bleeding. His voice had been sharp with fear, gentler with every word he didn't say.

Then the scene shifted — the Shrouded Vale, Eldrin before her, opening the secret passage as the nemods howled behind them. She'd felt his hand pull hers into the light, the first breath of safety after endless running.

The memory twisted again — the cliff's edge in the Dragon Graveyard; the sky falling away. She saw herself cutting the bandages from her wings, leaping into the abyss to save him.

And then — Drelf soil beneath her feet, the roar of battle fading to silence. Eldrin's hand in hers, trembling, his eyes steady and searching. Their breaths mingled; their hearts had understood what their lips never spoke. His thumb brushed her knuckles, grounding her, claiming nothing — yet promising everything.

"No!" Lyria gasped, reaching for him as the moment bled away.

The Sage tore it free.

Agony ripped through her chest, hollowing her from within. Her wings flared wide, silver fire racing through the veins of her mark as if it, too, resisted — but even that light dimmed. The warmth faded. The name faded. The *meaning* of him slipped like sand through her grasp.

Where love had burned, only ache remained — a wound with no shape.

She stumbled, Kaelis catching her, eyes wide with alarm. "What did it take?"

Lyria blinked through tears. Her lips moved, searching for a name that no longer lived there. Nothing came. No memory. No warmth. Only emptiness where something precious had been.

Her voice trembled. "I… don't know. Only that it mattered."

The Tree Sage's roots unfurled from her ankles, leaving her weak-kneed and shaking. Its ancient eyes glowed like lanterns deep within bark.

"The path is open," it intoned, voice deep as shifting stone. "Beneath the Umbrin's camp, roots hollow the earth. Follow them, and you will find the chains you seek to break."

Gravorn bent low, embers flickering in his gaze. "How long do we have?"

The Sage's branches creaked, a sound like old bones splitting. "The tunnels will close when the sun falls. If you have not returned by sunset, the earth will seal itself. None may follow — not you, not your foes. The shadows you sought to slay will bury you."

A ripple of unease passed through the group. Even the giants fell silent, their massive forms outlined in the flickering mist. The Sage's warning still hung in the air, heavy as stone.

Lyria's mark burned at her throat, but where it once drew strength from memory, only emptiness answered. The ache of loss was gone — replaced by something quieter, colder. She felt the drive to fight, to free those taken… but the face that once mattered most blurred, his memory slipping into shadow.

She lifted her chin, her voice steady but stripped of its old fire. "Then we waste no time. We prepare to strike."

Kaelis watched her a heartbeat too long. The same face, the same voice — but something in them rang hollow. The flame that once burned in Lyria's eyes now glinted like polished glass, bright but distant.

Kaelis said nothing. There was no time for doubt. But the silence between them felt different now — colder, heavier — as though something precious had been left behind in the roots.

The Tree Sage sank back into the soil, its form dissolving into the mist. Only its whisper lingered, curling through the silence. "Remember, child of storm: all gifts demand their cost."

Chapter 30

Eldrin's hand went to his side as the Aetherstone flamed— not with warmth, but with a cold so sharp it pierced straight through to the bone. He gasped, clutching at his ribs. Far below, the dagger answered, its hilt shuddering as faint white fire crawled along the blade. The reaction was violent, alive — as though something sacred had been torn away.

A hollow ache flooded his chest. Guilt struck like lightning, raw and blinding, so strong it nearly drove him to his knees. He felt it — the loss — sharp as a blade carving through his very soul. Something precious had been ripped from the weave that bound him to the world.

Lyria.

Their connection severed.

It slipped through his mind like a dying flame — burning once before vanishing into shadow. His grip tightened around the Aetherstone until his knuckles whitened. The stone pulsed harder, colder, like a heartbeat in mourning.

Camyra's voice coiled around him, soft and suffocating. "Say the words, Eldrin," she whispered, her golden hair brushing his cheek. "Vow yourself to me, and all chains will fall away. No king. No burden. No mark. Only freedom. Only us."

He turned on her — faster than she expected — eyes wild, breath ragged. "What did you do?"

Her lips parted, surprise flashing before smoothing into a smile. "Do?"

"The stone…" he hissed, pressing a trembling hand to his side. "It cried out. I felt her—and then she was gone. Don't lie to me."

Camyra tilted her head, feigning confusion. "You speak of ghosts, my love. Shadows in your mind."

Eldrin stepped closer, fury trembling through him. The dagger below glowed faintly, its white fire mirrored in his eyes. "You're the shadow," he said, voice rough. "You—"

Her fingers brushed his jaw, halting the words. "Anger suits you, my brave warrior," she murmured, her eyes shimmering with blue fire. "But it blinds you. Let it burn away the guilt, and you'll find peace."

The Aetherstone pulsed once—cold as ice. For a heartbeat, he saw her for what she was: beauty wrapped in shadow. Then the vision slid away beneath her smile.

"Say the words, Eldrin," Camyra whispered, her breath cool as shadow. "Let me take the ache away."

Finnian's shout cracked the air. He gripped the cage bars, knuckles white. "Don't you dare give yourself to her! She's not freedom—she's the chain!"

Camyra turned slowly, her smile like fire slicing silk. "Ah, the loyal one," she murmured. "Always watching. Always wanting. But never chosen."

Finnian's jaw tightened. "You'll kill him with your lies!"

"Lies?" Her voice dripped sweetness. "Or truth you're too afraid to face?"

Above, Thalendir's voice cut cold and clear. "Brother! You'll damn us all if you listen to her. Remember who you are. Remember your blood!"

The words hit like arrows. Eldrin flinched, his eyes sharpened—anger breaking through the haze. The Aetherstone throbbed under his ribs; the dagger burned below, a counter-rhythm to her spell.

Lyria's name pulsed faintly through the noise— distant, fading, but alive.

Camyra's laughter rippled softly and cruelly. "Listen to them," she said, turning back to him. "The brother who resents you. The friend who envies you. They would tear you apart if they could."

Her hand rose, palm hovering just over his chest. "You don't need them, Eldrin. You only need me. Choose me, and you'll never feel loss again."

For an instant, the air stilled—heat and cold clashing, light and shadow coiling. The Aetherstone pulsed once, sharp as pain.

Finnian slammed the cage bars. "She's feeding on you, Eldrin! She's feeding on everything you are!"

Camyra's tone turned knife-sharp. "Feeding? I give *him* power! I offer him what none of you could—freedom from the chains of duty and sorrow!"

Her gaze flicked to Finnian, voice lowering to a purr. "You would take that power if you could. You burn every time I touch him."

Finnian froze, fury and shame warring across his face.

"Enough!" Thalendir roared. "Enough of your venom, witch!"

Camyra smiled, unshaken. "See, Eldrin? They fear you. They always have. You are stronger alone."

The dagger flared in answer, a surge of white fire that split the air. The Aetherstone burned cold beneath his palm, the two forces warring through him—light against the lure of shadow.

But this time, he did not falter.

Eldrin's jaw tightened, his voice raw but steady. "You don't know me," he said, forcing each word past the pressure of her spell. "And you'll never have what I am."

For the first time, Camyra's smile slipped.

The dagger's light cut through her illusion, scattering her glamour like torn smoke. The chains rattled as Eldrin straightened, breath shuddering but defiant.

Camyra hissed softly, the sound serpentine. "You'll regret that."

"Maybe," he said, eyes blazing with the dagger's reflection. "But not today."

From the far edge of the firelight, a low chuckle slithered through the dark.

Drakor.

His crooked wings flexed, stirring ash into the air. The fire spat and hissed, sparks scattering across the ground like fleeing stars. Jagged shadows crawled over his scales, over claw and fang, until only his eyes burned through—the molten hue of dying embers refusing to fade.

"The elf resists," he rasped, his grin widening, fractured and cruel. "But it won't matter. Her magic coils tighter with every breath."

He leaned forward, the heat warping the air around him. "Soon the bond will break him… and the mark will be mine."

The last words rolled like smoke, heavy with hunger. A flicker of flame caught along his teeth as he smiled, and the night itself seemed to recoil.

Drovane's gaze flicked to him, sharp as a blade drawn in silence. "Yours?" His lips curved into a smile that never reached his eyes. "Shadow claims what fire cannot. When he falls, it will be to the nighborn."

The crooked dragon's wings twitched. For a heartbeat, the two predators stared across the firelight, neither yielding.

From the dark behind them, Zyressa's head lifted. Smoke curled from her nostrils as she leaned close to Velthar, her words only a growl beneath the crackle of flame.

"Let them quarrel like pups. Drakor and the elf think the mark is theirs. But it is not for them to keep."

Velthar's tail carved a slow furrow in the dirt, his eyes never leaving Eldrin's cage. His voice rumbled back, low, certain. "Yes.... Let them tear at each other. When the mark burns, it will not shine for crooked wings or empty shadows. It will bow to us."

Zyressa's muzzle curved into something that might have been a smile, though it held no warmth. "Then we wait. And when the moment comes… we take it. All of it."

Their eyes gleamed in the dark, reflecting the fire. Silent. Patient. Already imagining betrayal.

Chapter 31

The land grew harsher as they pressed west; the mountains sagged behind them, and the dark green of the Arden gathered ahead. The air was heavier here—wet with rot, tasting faintly of ash.

Aldareth raised a hand at the tree line, bringing the column to a halt. Hooves shifted restlessly on the uneven ground, breath steaming in the chill. His jaw set as he studied the shadowed expanse.

"The Arden," he said at last. Naming it felt like inviting danger.

This forest was not their own. The canopy knotted thick, dark trunks hunched low under heavy limbs that reached for the ground. Wind moved through them without stirring a single leaf, whispering from nowhere.

Aerion's bow creaked softly as she notched an arrow, her mare sidestepping beneath her. "So, this is where the Nightborn hide."

Aelar tightened his hold on his reins, voice quiet but steady. "And where we defeat them."

Caelith's fire dimmed for once. He stroked his mount's neck, feeling the tension coil in the animal's muscles. "I don't like riding into shadow. But if the king's sons are there…" His gaze flicked ahead. "We go."

Aldareth's eyes narrowed. "Stay sharp," he said at last. "The Arden is not only watched by eyes. The forest itself watches. Whatever walks here may be allied with the Umbrin."

He urged his gelding forward, and the others followed, crossing the threshold into shadow. The trees closed overhead, blotting out what little light remained. The air pressed close, thick with damp and rot.

A storm of blackbirds erupted from the underbrush—wings like torn cloth, cries scraping the silence raw. The horses reared and snorted, ears pinned, hooves striking sparks against stone. Steel rasped half free, bowstrings groaned. Then the flock vanished, and a faint laugh slithered between the trunks—too near for chance, not wholly beast, not wholly elf.

The laugh died into silence, but the forest did not return to stillness. Every branch seemed to hold its breath.

Aerion's bow rose; her arrow aimed into the black trunks. "We're not alone."

A shadow detached from the undergrowth as the echo of that strange laugh still lingered. The horses sidestepped, snorting softly, their reins creaking under white-knuckled grips. Steel whispered from scabbards in one fluid motion.

Aldareth steadied his mount with a low murmur, then urged it half a step forward, sword angled low, voice steady.

"Show yourself!"

The figure moved with the silence of something born to the dark — its shadow-cloak mottled in grays and greens that blurred with the forest floor. A faint glimmer caught the light where the hood slipped back: scaled ridges along his jaw and forearms, like the ghost of armor fused with flesh. His green drelf eyes glinted, veined with silver, sharp as knives and always searching.

"You'll find no sport in pointing steel at me," he said, tone dry, edged with mockery. "If I meant you harm, you'd already be bleeding." A sinuous tail flicked behind him.

Aerion's arrow held steady. "And if we meant you harm, you'd already be dead."

The stranger's mouth curved faintly — not quite a smile. "Fair enough. But you're far from your precious citadel, and these woods do not forgive strays." His gaze shifted deliberately to Aldareth. "I am Zeynar. Nyxari sent me. She said you might need a guide who knows the Arden's teeth better than most."

Aldareth's grip eased, though his eyes stayed hard. "She said nothing about sending another."

"No," Zeynar said, stepping closer, movements smooth and reptilian. "But then, Nyxari doesn't say everything, does she?" His eyes flicked to the canopy above. "You'll want to keep moving. The Arden listens. The longer you linger, the more it decides whether you're prey or not."

The elves exchanged brief, wary looks. One of the horses stamped, tossing its mane as if agreeing with them.

"Lead, then," Aldareth said at last, his tone like tempered steel. "But know this — if your path takes us astray, it will be your life spent for it."

Zeynar inclined his head, not offended but faintly amused. "Spoken like an elf. Always noble threats." His pale eyes cut toward the depths of the forest. "Come. I'll show you the way. Try to keep up."

He moved off, low and fluid, a predator slipping between roots and shadow.

Caelith's jaw tightened, but he said nothing. Aerion lowered her bow just enough to signal restraint, though her eyes never left the drelf. The mounts shifted uneasily as the darkness thickened, their hooves muffled by damp earth.

For a breath, the elves stayed motionless — four riders balanced on the edge of mistrust — then Aldareth nodded once, curt and decisive.

"Stay sharp," he said. "We follow."

And together, they urged their mounts forward and plunged after Zeynar into the waiting Arden.

Below, the faint orange glow of firelight shimmered through the trees. The Umbrin camp breathed like an animal — shadows drifting, laughter stitched with the click of metal. From the far side of the ravine came the low earth-hum of something vast, waiting. Between those lights and that hush, the Arden held its breath.

Aldareth drew his horse to a halt behind a screen of twisted roots, the animal's breath steaming in the cold. He scanned the slope below, his jaw tight. "There," he murmured. "Their fires. The Umbrin camp."

Zeynar crouched low beside him, his scaled markings catching stray glimmers as he peered downslope. "We're close," he whispered. "Closer than is safe."

The elves reined in their mounts, the horses stamping softly, nostrils flaring at the strange scent of smoke and shadow. Aerion eased her bowstring back, eyes narrowing toward the flicker of campfires. "Then this is where we wait?"

But Zeynar's nostrils flared, his gaze shifting. He stilled. "Maybe. But look… there."

The elves followed his line of sight. Through the drifting mist, vast silhouettes moved between the trees — shapes too large, too slow, eyes glowing faintly.

Caelith's hand tightened on his reins. "Giants?"

Zeynar's grip closed around his sword, his voice low, edged with something almost like respect. "So, they honored the oath," he murmured. "Good. We will need their strength."

Aldareth's gaze swept the ravine again, lingering on the enemy fires, then the dark figures preparing to strike. He could almost feel it — the pull of prophecy, the mark burning somewhere beyond that light.

Nyxari's warning echoed in his mind: *Chains of shadow cannot be cut by steel. Only the dagger can break what binds him.*

"But where are the drelves? And the others?" Aelar asked, voice low. "We need to be certain of their positions before we move."

Zeynar's eyes caught the faint firelight, sharp as glass. He didn't disagree — but in the Arden, hesitation was just another way of dying.

Chapter 32

Beneath the Arden, the tunnels pressed close — damp, narrow veins of earth that pulsed faintly with root-light. Lyria crouched near the opening, Kaelis beside her, the air trembling with the distant rumble of giants shifting above the ridge.

In the flickering green glow, the skitterling squirmed in Kaelis's grip — a wiry creature with slick scales and too many teeth. It hissed, snapping at her fingers, its eyes rolling with panic.

Kaelis scowled. "Are you sure this will work?"

Lyria's mouth curved faintly. "Yes. It'll run to the dragon that sent it… weaving through the camp and lighting everything in its path."

She lifted a small oil-soaked rag and tied it to the creature's tail with a strip of cloth. The skitterling shrieked and thrashed harder, claws scraping the air.

Kaelis muttered a curse. "You're either insane or a genius."

Lyria's eyes glinted. "Desperate," she corrected.

Kaelis lit the rag and, with a sharp shove, released the skitterling. The creature bolted down the tunnel, claws clattering, tail ablaze. The flickering light darted through the dark like a comet gone mad.

Above them, Gravorn's voice rumbled from the ridge, deep as thunder. "When the fire rises," he called down, "we descend as storm."

Kaelis exhaled, wings flexing against the tunnel's narrow walls. "Ready to fly?"

Lyria's smirk widened. "Ready."

A heartbeat later, a shriek split the night — followed by a *whoosh* of igniting pitch.

Then another.

And another.

Fire exploded through the lower camp, racing up tents and trees in a line of chaotic brilliance. The skitterling, now a streak of terror and flame, darted wildly through the Umbrin ranks — spreading destruction far beyond what even Lyria imagined. The blaze caught the tar pits, igniting them in bursts of molten light.

Smoke rose thick as thunderclouds. From the ridge, the giants roared in answer, hurling boulders into the fire-lit camp. Each strike shook the ground, scattering the Umbrin into panic.

The nightborn shouted in confusion — half dousing flames, half striking at shadows that danced and split like living fire. The camp dissolved into chaos.

Above it all, wings unfolded.

Lyria and Kaelis rose together, smoke and wind surging beneath them, blades catching the light as they drove through the haze. Firelight limned their armor, their descent timed perfectly with the giants' charge from the ridge above.

From the tunnels below, the war-band of elves and drelves poured forth—steel flashing, tails waving like banners in the updraft of flame.

And from the ridge, the thunder of hooves shattered the roar of fire. Aldareth's elves burst from the smoke—mounted and armored, their formation cutting through the inferno like a storm unleashed. Their war cries rose to meet the clash of steel, answering darkness with fury.

Zeynar dove from the rim, wings snapping wide, his descent a streak of shadow and flame. He struck the camp like a blade from the sky, knives flashing as he tore through the first ranks of Umbrin, his roar merging with the thunder of the charge below.

The war for the captives had begun.

Flames writhed between the trees, the camp now a storm without a center.

High above, the cages swayed — massive knots of rope suspended from the blackened canopy, creaking under heat and strain. Inside them, Eldrin, Thalendir, and Finnian clung to the bars as the forest burned around them.

"Cut the ropes!" Aldareth's voice carried up from below, rough and commanding as his horse plunged through the smoke, embers swirling around him like sparks from a forge.

Zeynar's tail lashed as he caught sight of the cages. "I see them."

The group split without hesitation — Aerion's bow sang, arrows slicing through the haze to drive back Umbrin sentries. At the tree's base, Caelith and Aelar wheeled their mounts into the fray, blades flashing, carving space for the others to move. Sparks burst like stars as steel met steel, the elves fighting with fierce precision while Zeynar banked, wings flaring wide. His knives gleamed in the firelight as he slashed through the first knot of ropes.

Thalendir's cage lurched, ropes snapping one by one with sharp cracks. The entire structure pitched into the open air. The prince braced for the ground rushing up beneath him — but a dark shape swept past. Zeynar's wings flared, his arms hooking under Thalendir's shoulders. The impact still jarred, knocking the breath from his chest, but the drelf slowed the fall, easing him into a controlled crash instead of a killing one.

They struck the ground, rolling through ash and splintered wood. Thalendir staggered upright, chest heaving, teeth bared. “I had it,” he growled.

Zeynar’s smirk was sharp. “Of course you did. Try not to die proving it.” His eyes flicked upward, already fixed on the next cage. He launched skyward again, wings beating against the smoke.

Finnian’s prison swung wildly above the blaze. One rope had already frayed to strands; another snapped with a sound like a whip. The cage tilted violently, spilling him against the bars. He caught himself on the edge with one hand, his body dangling as the rope fibers groaned, ready to give way.

“Little help here?” he shouted, sweat and smoke stinging his eyes. His grip tightened on the rope.

The drelf angled toward him, tail lashing for balance, but the cage swung like a pendulum between the trees, keeping Finnian just out of reach.

“Hold on!” Zeynar shouted.

He dove again, wings cutting through smoke and ash, claws outstretched. The final rope snapped with a sound like a whip, and Finnian was suddenly weightless — flung into open air. The world spun, sky and fire trading places as he fell.

Zeynar’s wings cracked open, the gust nearly hurling him backward, but he forced the dive steeper. The wind howled in his ears. “Reach for me!”

Finnian's hand shot out, fingers brushing empty space once—twice—then caught on a scaled foot slick with blood and soot as it curled around his fingers. For a heartbeat, their grips slid, the air tearing at them, threatening to wrench them apart.

Zeynar snarled, muscles straining as his claws dug deep. "Hold on!"

Their hold locked again—barely. The drelf's wings flared, slowing the fall just enough to twist them from a deadly plunge into a crashing glide. The impact hit like a hammer; they rolled through dirt and embers, skidding across scorched ground before coming to a breathless halt.

Smoke curled around them. Zeynar's chest heaved, one wing dragging, torn at the edge. Finnian coughed hard, spitting ash, his hand still gripping Zeynar's toes in disbelief that he was alive.

Zeynar managed a rough, breathless grin. "Next time," he rasped, "I'll teach you how to land."

Finnian coughed, dragging himself upright, just as an Umbrin lunged from the haze. With no blade in hand, he ducked under the slash and drove his fist into the dark elf's ribs. The two crashed into the dirt, grappling among sparks and embers. Finnian seized a shard of broken wood and rammed it into his foe's throat. The Umbrin collapsed with a choking gasp.

A snarl split the smoke — a shadow lunged for Thalendir a few feet away. He caught the strike on his forearm, turning with the blow instead of resisting it. In one fluid motion, he twisted the Umbrin's wrist, sending the dagger clattering free, then pivoted on his heel and drove an open-handed strike beneath its jaw. The creature staggered back, collapsing into the wreckage without a sound.

Zeynar joined the fray, his sword a blur. He cut down another nightborn, padded feet crushing ash as he shoved the body aside. "Find your steel," he barked at the newly released captives. "You'll need it."

Finnian and Thalendir scattered through the wreckage, kicking aside shattered crates and broken beams. Then Finnian froze, a grin breaking through blood and soot. A gleam of steel winked up at him from the ash. He tore free his twin swords, blades catching firelight as if they'd been waiting for his hands.

"Much better," he muttered, spinning them in unison.

Thalendir shoved aside a fallen beam, his hand closing around the familiar hilt of his sword. He ripped it free, swinging once to test the balance. The steel hissed through the air, and his eyes burned with grim fire.

Above… the last cage groaned as the ropes stretched — Eldrin's.

But he was not alone.

A shimmer of gold and shadow wound its way to his prison, gliding through firelight like a song given form.

Camyra.

Her hand brushed the ropes. Runes flared along her fingers, whispering as they unspooled the knots. The bindings loosened, the door creaking open.

"Come," she urged softly. "The path is open, Eldrin. Leave this fire. Leave the burden. Come with me, and you will be free."

Eldrin's fingers tightened around the bars. His heart pounded, not with longing—but with warning. Below, his dagger lay amid the churned mud, its blade catching the flames and gleaming white-hot for an instant, as though alive.

His voice came rough but steady. "Not without my blade."

Camyra's eyes narrowed, her smile faltering for the first time. "That dagger chains you to prophecy," she whispered, each word sliding like silk over glass. "You don't need it. You don't need *them*."

She leaned closer, golden hair brushing the bars, her breath cold against his cheek. "Come with me, Eldrin. You've fought long enough. Let it end."

For a moment, the air pulsed between them—her sorcery pressing against his will like a tide against rock. The Aetherstone flared under his ribs, answering the dagger's glow below.

His jaw clenched. "I don't run from fire," he said, forcing each word through the weight of her spell. "I fight through it."

Camyra's eyes flashed—half fury, half fascination. "You think you still have a choice?"

"I *make* my choice."

Below, Thalendir cut through the melee, sword slick with blood and ash. His eyes locked on the golden-haired enchantress, on the way her hand lingered at Eldrin's face. For a breath, his steps faltered—until he saw the defiance burning in his brother's eyes.

"Brother, let's go!" he roared, his voice tearing through the din.

Nearby, Finnian fought like a storm, twin blades cutting through Umbrin ranks. "Eldrin!" he shouted. "We need your help!!"

Camyra's expression hardened, her glamour rippling. "They'll die here," she hissed. "All of them. And for what?"

The ground trembled beneath them. A new sound rolled through the forest—low, guttural, ancient. The trees shuddered.

Camyra turned toward the dark, her smile curving slowly and knowingly. "Ahhh…" she murmured, voice laced with anticipation.

"He rises."

The flames bent, drawn toward a gathering heat that split the air with a hiss of sulfur. Shadows deepened to black, devouring the light.

Then came the roar—vast and deafening, a sound that seemed to tear the very breath from the world.

Drakor.

He burst from the heart of the firestorm—crooked wings unfurling, scales cracked and burning with veins of molten gold. His body was ruined made flesh, but his fury made him magnificent. Fire poured from his jaws in a torrent of gold and black, scorching sky and soil alike.

Camyra's hair whipped in the heat, her eyes alight—not with command, but with hunger. "Yes," she breathed. "Feed on it. Feed on my power."

The flames surged higher, drawn to her glow. Drakor's head turned, sensing her presence—the power radiating from her like sunlight through poison. His wings flexed, drinking in the magic that bled from her, and his roar split the night once more, louder, wilder.

He was not hers to command.

But her darkness made him strong.

And together, they burned.

Kaelis wheeled aside Lyria, her Shadowcloak flaring dark across her wings. For an instant, she vanished into smoke — but her heart still thundered, hot with rage. The cloak shimmered, flickered, and betrayed her, a faint outline gleaming where it should have hidden her.

Drakor saw.

He turned with a snarl, flame igniting in his throat. Kaelis dove, heat grazing her wingtips as the firestorm rolled past. Below, the elves scattered for cover, the giants bracing as the dragon's shadow tore across the ridge. His fire struck the clearing, searing the air in a storm of molten wind.

And through that chaos, two figures cut through the haze.

Kaelis climbed higher, wings beating hard, the edges of her cloak smoking where dragon fire had kissed it. Below her, Lyria burst through the ash — silver flame racing along the mark at her throat, the cloak about her shoulders alive with shifting shadow.

"There you are, you wretched beast," she hissed, diving low.

Drakor turned, eyes narrowing. He saw her — saw the mark burning bright against the storm — and lunged.

Fire poured from his jaws. Lyria banked sharply, the Shadowcloak wrapping her in living smoke, deflecting most of the blaze. But her fury broke her focus, and the magic faltered. For an instant, her light flared through the shroud — blindingly bright, exposed.

Drakor roared and struck.

Kaelis dove to intercept, her blade flashing, but the dragon's wing swept through the air like a hammer, hurling her back into the smoke.

And through the torrent of flame and ash, Lyria rose again.

Her cloak snapped wide, now half-light, half-shadow — one side devouring the air, the other blazing silver-white. The mark burned like a fallen star. Its light seared the dragon's gaze, dragging it away from Kaelis. Drakor's pupils narrowed — recognition, hatred, hunger — and then he surged upward.

Lyria met him midair.

Claws clashed against scales, wings struck wings — the sound was thunder made flesh. The mark's radiance scorched his hide, staggering him but not breaking him. He roared, the sound shaking the forest as sparks and cinders rained like burning snow.

Below, elves and drelves looked up in awe and terror, the sky split with shadow and silver fire — one drelf's fury against the dark.

For a heartbeat, the heavens belonged to them — Lyria's radiance clashing with Drakor's flame, Kaelis diving from the clouds to strike and vanish again. Below, the forest blazed. Giants moved through smoke and fire like mountains come alive, their silhouettes wreathed in embers.

Then the sky deepened — and grew dark.

Two vast forms broke through the storm above, wings blotting out the sky. Zyressa and Velthar — emerald and bronze, gleaming in the inferno — circled like vultures over a dying world. Their eyes reflected the flames below: watching, waiting, judging when to strike.

The giants saw them.

Gravorn's roar split the air — deep as stone cracking, ancient as thunder. "Now!"

The ridge shook as the giants heaved. Boulders the size of towers ripped from the earth, glowing orange as they caught the firelight.

The first rock hurtled past Zyressa, close enough that the wind of its passing tore scales from her flank. She shrieked, wings twisting, smoke trailing in her wake.

The second found its mark.

Velthar's scream split the heavens as stone met flesh and fire. His wing folded with a crack like mountains breaking. He spiraled downward — a comet of bronze and flame — tearing through canopy and camp alike. Trees exploded. Umbrin scattered. The ground convulsed beneath the impact.

For a single breath, the battlefield froze.

Then chaos returned tenfold. Velthar's body crashed through the camp, his tail carving trenches through tents and towers before going still. The shockwave sent elves, drelves, and Umbrin reeling. Fire bloomed in waves across the ridge.

Above, Lyria steadied herself, wings trembling against the rising heat. Drakor reeled midair, one slit eye flicking toward the fallen dragon — fury there, yes, but something else glimmered too. Shock. And the faintest sliver of fear.

The Shadowcloak around Lyria flickered, responding to the storm inside her — pride, pain, and something hollow she could not name. The mark burned bright, defiant, while below the battlefield seemed to hold its breath.

Then Zyressa screamed — a sound of pure vengeance.

She dove, emerald wings slicing the smoke, her roar a promise to shatter mountains.

And in the smoke below, Drovane moved.

He could see the battle turning — dragons falling, flames consuming the camp — and he would not be left powerless when the smoke cleared. The Umbrin spymaster slipped between wreckage and flame, a shadow made flesh, eyes fixed on the dagger gleaming faintly in the dirt.

Each step was soundless. Each breath measured. The blade's light painted his face in pale fire as he reached for it — quick as a serpent striking — even as, above him, Eldrin clung to the open cage, torn between Camyra's outstretched hand and his brother's voice shouting through the roar.

Eldrin snapped out of the trance long enough to see Drovane closing in.

"The dagger! Stop him!"

Finnian glanced up, then followed Eldrin's finger to the ground. He sprinted through the haze, twin blades flashing. Drovane whirled at the shout, his hood thrown back, eyes burning with silver-veined malice. A curved dagger gleamed in his grip, wicked as a fang.

Steel clashed in a spray of sparks. Drovane struck fast, every blow angled toward keeping Finnian from the dagger on the ground between them. Finnian pressed hard, both blades moving as one — a blur of feints and cuts — but the spymaster was quick. He slid low, his strike grazing Finnian's leg before twisting away.

"You don't deserve such power," Drovane hissed, his voice as sharp as his knife. "Better in my hand than wasted on you."

Finnian's grin flashed through the soot. "We'll see about that." He parried high, spun low, and pressed harder, driving the Umbrin back. His swords carved bright arcs through the fire-lit haze.

Drovane lashed out suddenly, sweeping a kick at Finnian's legs. The elf vaulted over it, twisting midair, blades striking down. One sliced across Drovane's arm — shallow, but enough to stagger him.

The spymaster fell to one knee, his hand still clawing for the dagger in the dirt.

Finnian's boot pinned it out of reach. His blades crossed in a scissor at Drovane's throat.

"Not yours," Finnian growled and drove steel home.

Drovane choked once, black blood spilling across the ash, then toppled into the dirt. The fire swallowed his shadow, but the battlefield gave no pause.

Above the burning camp, the sky writhed with wings and fire.

Lyria's mark blazed, silver light slashing through the smoke as she met Drakor's onslaught head-on. Her claws raked his twisted scales, sparks showering through the haze. His roar split the heavens — a furnace of fury and flame — every beat of his wings scattering storms across the Arden.

Kaelis darted through the smoke beside her, a streak of shadow and steel. Her Shadowcloak rippled around her like living night, turning her strikes into blurs of darkness. She slashed across Drakor's flank, carving deep, smoking grooves, before veering away again.

"He's faltering!" she shouted — but even as the words left her lips, Drakor's tail lashed. The blow caught her wing, hurling her sideways through the haze.

Lyria dove after her, the mark blazing hotter with every heartbeat. Silver fire streamed from her hands as she forced herself between Drakor's jaws and her friend. The cloak at her shoulders flared wide — a storm of living smoke and light — wrapping them both in shifting darkness.

The dragon's fire struck, roaring across the cloak's folds. For a heartbeat, it held — a shroud of protection, swallowing flame. Then emotion broke through. Lyria's fury. Her fear. Her loss.

The cloak shuddered.

Where shadow had once obeyed, it rebelled, tendrils lashing outward like anger given form. Light and dark tangled, the edge of her own power turning against her. The heat seared her skin; the air screamed with pressure.

Kaelis's voice broke through the chaos, hoarse and urgent. "Lyria — control it!"

But Lyria couldn't. The mark flared too bright, too wild. It wanted to burn everything — to fill the emptiness left inside her by a memory she couldn't name.

The cloak split.

Half shadow, half flame, it tore through the air around her, scattering embers like falling stars. Lyria screamed, driving herself upward, meeting Drakor's claws with her own. The impact cracked like thunder.

Her light met his fire — silver and black colliding — and the sky shuddered under the weight of it.

Below, the armies looked up to see gods in battle: a silver-winged fury locked against a dragon of ruin, the dark itself bleeding light.

And then, from above, a roar far greater split the sky.

Zyressa.

She burst through the smoke, a comet of emerald flame cutting across the heavens. Her cry tore through the clouds, a sound of rage and grief entwined — vengeance made flesh. She dove for the ridge, for Gravorn and the giants who had slain Velthar.

Drakor's head snapped toward the sound. His breath hitched mid-roar, the flames at his throat faltering. For one heartbeat, his fury turned elsewhere.

Lyria *felt* that weakness — and something inside her, hollow and aching, surged against it. The mark at her throat blazed, flooding her veins with silver light. She didn't understand why it hurt so much to burn. She didn't remember *who* it was for. But she knew this: she could not stop.

She struck.

Wings snapped open, cutting through smoke. Her claws tore across Drakor's neck, light searing shadow. His bellow split the clouds, fire raining from his jaws as the force of their collision sent them both spinning through the storm.

Below, the giants bellowed their answer. Gravorn lifted another boulder, his massive shoulders straining, and hurled it skyward. More followed, stones arcing like meteors into the darkening air. One missed wide; another struck Zyressa's wing, sending her reeling before she caught herself, fury turning her flight into fire as she spun out of control.

Down through the haze, the stricken dragon fell, wings folding like broken sails. She struck the ridge— Fire and stone collided, the explosion consuming her in a storm that shook the Arden to its roots.

The light was bleeding from the sky now. The sun slipped lower, its gold fading to blood-red. Shadows stretched long through the Arden, and the first fingers of dusk curled around the battlefield.

The tunnels would not remain open much longer.

Time was slipping away…

Chapter 33

The fire raged, but Eldrin heard nothing.

Below, the world burned—dragons twisting through smoke, giants hurling stone, fire, and shadow, tearing the sky apart. But all he saw was *her*.

A flash of silver-white wings against the blaze.

Lyria.

Her light cut through the storm like a blade, striking again and again at the crooked form of Drakor. Kaelis wheeled beside her, fierce and fast, their movements in perfect rhythm—two warriors moving as one.

Something inside Eldrin stirred—an ache so deep it left him breathless. The Aetherstone burned at his side, beating in time with his heart.

Beside him, Camyra's hand lingered on the open cage. Her gaze followed his, tracing the line of his sight to the silver-winged figure battling the dragon. Her smile curved—beautiful, venomous.

"So that's what binds you," she murmured. "That spark you would burn for."

Eldrin's grip tightened on the bars. The Aetherstone throbbed harder—a desperate pulse, a warning. Below, half-buried in ash and shadow, the dagger flickered faintly, its glow dimming as the sun bled into the horizon.

Camyra raised her hand, her voice dropping to a whisper that slid through the smoke like a blade drawn in silk.

"Rhaegorath," she breathed.

The air shivered.

Then trembled.

A low, guttural sound rose from the depths below—half roar, half groan—as if something vast and ancient stirred in answer. The ground quaked beneath them. Chains of magic rippled through the air, unseen but felt, winding like serpents across the battlefield.

Eldrin's breath caught.

Camyra's eyes burned like twin embers through the smoke.

The ground split.

And from the fractures, wings unfurled—vast and black as cinder, the air bending beneath their span. Firelight raced along their edges, only to vanish as the scales drank the glow, devouring it whole.

Rhaegorath rose.

He was not like the others. This dragon was bound—his body a vessel of her summoning, his eyes burning with black enchantment.

His roar shattered the air, scattering the Umbrin ranks and sending Eldrin's cage lurching on its chain.

Camyra's hair whipped in the rising wind, her voice low, exultant.
"Let her light meet mine," she whispered. "And see which flame the world remembers."

Rhaegorath's answering scream tore the clouds apart. His wings blotted out the sky as he surged upward, fire pouring from his throat in a torrent that turned the air itself to flame.

Lyria reeled mid-flight as the heat struck her, the mark at her throat searing like molten iron. She banked hard, wings cutting through the roiling air, her chest heaving against the smoke. The light of her mark wavered, silver fracturing under gold.

The black dragon was closing in.

Its wings cleaved the air with a sound like breaking mountains. Each beat sent shockwaves through the storm, scattering ash and embers across the ridge. Lyria dove, shadow and fire chasing her through the night. Her mark blazed in answer—defiant, desperate.

Beside her, Kaelis's Shadowcloak rippled, flickering between concealment and flame. Fear made the magic unstable. Rage made it visible. Every surge of emotion drew the fire closer.

"Keep your focus!" Kaelis shouted, her voice raw over the roar. "He's hunting the light—don't let it find you!"

But the black dragon's eyes had already locked on the glow burning beneath Lyria's throat.

Camyra stood atop Eldrin's cage, hand raised, her eyes burning the same black fire as the beast she commanded. Her voice rolled across the battlefield—a whisper and a spell entwined.

"Destroy her," she breathed. "Extinguish her light."

Below, the battlefield froze. Even the giants stilled as the creature folded its wings and dove—smoke, fire, and command woven into one terrible descent.

And above it all, Drakor watched.

Through the torn clouds, his eyes narrowed, smoke curling from his nostrils. The black dragon was not his spawn—its scent wrong, its magic fouled—but it answered a voice he knew. A voice steeped in the same dark promise that had once bound him to Vartharax's will.

He bared his jagged teeth. *So… the wraith calls her pet.*

Lyria's silver light flared—the mark answering with the last of her strength, defiance pulsing through exhaustion.

Drakor's hatred boiled over. The mark. The prophecy. Her wings. Every shimmer of silver was a reminder of his failure, of what Vartharax had demanded—and what he had not delivered.

He beat his crooked wings, roaring, his voice splitting the clouds. "She must die."

Two dragons turned as one. Fire met fire, darkness met light. Their twin torrents of flame spiraled downward, merging into a storm that could consume the sky itself.

And caught within that storm—two drelves, their Shadowcloaks flickering like torn veils—fought not to vanish with it.

Drakor beat his wings, roaring. Two against one. *Let the skies burn clean.*

The black dragon heard him and turned in tandem, its fire swirling into his twin torrents of flame spiraling toward Lyria and Kaelis.

Lyria's mark flamed in one desperate burst, but even that light faltered.

Eldrin's heart seized. The Aetherstone throbbed violently in his palm.

"Stop it!" he roared, seizing Carmyra's wrist. "Call them off!"

Her head turned, her smile soft—and cruel.

"Why? This is the end you asked for," she whispered. "Freedom."

"Freedom?" His voice cracked. "You call this freedom?"

The words hung between them, swallowed by the roar of fire and the dying sun. Around them, the battlefield seemed to slow— the air itself thick with ash and despair.

The sun slipped lower, its last gold bleeding into blood-red dusk. Shadows stretched long across the battlefield.

And in that deepening dark, the dagger stirred. Its light seared through the smoke—white and alive—brighter than it had burned since Eldrin first carried it.

The Aetherstone at Eldrin's side throbbed once—cold, pleading—as if something unseen still fought to reach him.

Near the edge of the chaos, Zeynar felt the surge. He spun, eyes flaring in alarm.

"The dagger," he hissed to Finnian, who stood beside Drovane's fallen corpse. "It's calling to him. It's not just his weapon—it's the key. Only the dagger can destroy her hold."

Finnian's head snapped toward it. The blade glowed as if it breathed.

Above, Eldrin gripped the cage door, eyes locked on that same light. His lips parted—a whisper lost in the firestorm.

"My knife…"

Zeynar's voice rang out through the din like steel: "Get the blade!"

Finnian lunged. His boots pounded through ash, sparks bursting with every stride. He dropped to one knee, hand closing around the hilt—

—and Eldrin's breath caught.

No fire came.

Instead, the dagger's glow leapt up Finnian's arm—fierce, living—but not burning. For one stunned heartbeat, he froze, staring down at the steel blazing in his friend's grasp.

"Impossible," Eldrin breathed, voice breaking.

Carmyra's golden eyes flared, fury twisting her beauty. "No—!" Her hand sliced the air, shadows writhing from her fingertips. "It's not his to wield."

Finnian lifted the blade, breath ragged. Power surged through him—wild, ancient, unbound—threatening to tear him apart. He staggered, but held fast, light spilling from the steel.

And for an instant, across the chaos, three lights answered one another:

- Lyria's mark blazing in the sky,
- Eldrin's Aetherstone pulsing with icy fire,
- Finnian's arm trembling beneath the dagger's radiant glow.

The battlefield itself shuddered—as though prophecy had pressed its hand upon the world—

and the world had finally listened.

Finnian's chest clenched as he looked skyward through the rising smoke. The dagger's light brightened in his grasp, as if urging him to act.

"Eldrin!" he shouted.

Through the haze, their eyes met—a flicker of recognition amid chaos, a silent understanding that needed no words.

With a sharp twist of his arm, Finnian hurled the glowing blade skyward. It sliced through the smoke, turning end over end, its light catching on every arc. For a breathless moment, it hung there, spinning between fire and ash—

Then flew true, reaching for its master's outstretched hand.

Eldrin caught it through the bars. The hilt struck his palm, nearly tearing free—then the steel ignited, bright as a star. The flare raced outward, colliding with Lyria's mark. A pulse of blinding power struck both dragons, light tearing across their scales as the blast hurled them backward.

Lyria fell through the smoke, wings shuddering, spent from the release of power. Kaelis dove after her, catching her wrist just before the ground could claim her.

Above, the flare faded from the sky—and in its wake, silence hung like a held breath.

Carmyra stood motionless inside the cage, firelight dancing across her face. Her eyes fixed on the dagger in Eldrin's hand—on the light still burning along its edge. For the first time, her expression faltered.

"You saved her." Her voice was soft, almost wonder-struck. "Even now… after all I've given you."

Eldrin's chest heaved. The Aetherstone at his side pulsed faintly, cold and alive.

"I had to," he said, his voice rough. He met her gaze, unflinching.

"I love her."

Chapter 34

Camyra stepped closer, the ropes between them casting black ribbons across her skin.

The air shuddered.

Her gaze lifted toward the horizon. Toward Lyria.

"She must burn," she whispered—her voice swelling, resonant now with something vast and dangerous.

She extended her hand toward the sky.

From the clouds above, a roar split the air—one voice, then another. The smoke parted as Drakor clawed his way back into the open, wings torn but burning with renewed fury. Beside him, the black dragon rose again from the ash, eyes glazed and glowing like twin suns of molten gold.

Both turned toward the same mark of light below. Lyria.

Camyra's voice rolled through the storm, silken and savage: "Finish her."

The command struck like thunder.

Drakor and the black dragon moved as one—wheeling high, then diving—two storms descending through the haze. Fire streamed from their jaws, converging into a single torrent that lit the forest like dawn.

Lyria looked up, breath catching. The heat blistered the air around her; Kaelis dove beside her, wings flaring wide, shielding what she could. The light was too bright, too near—

"No!" Eldrin roared. He slammed Camyra against the bars, his hand at her throat, the dagger trembling in his grasp.

She turned slowly, eyes molten, her smile a curve of hunger and triumph. "Swear yourself to me, and I will call them back."

Then—from below, through the roar of flame—a voice rose, hoarse and fierce:

"Eldrin, finish her!"

Finnian.

Lyria looked up, breath catching. The air blistered with heat, rippling around her. Kaelis dove beside her, wings flaring wide, shielding what she could. The light was too bright—too near—

"No!"

Eldrin's roar tore through the chaos. He slammed Camyra back against the bars, his hand locked around her throat, the dagger burning white in his grasp.

Her head tilted slowly, golden hair spilling like molten light. Her smile curved—not in fear, but in hunger. "Swear yourself to me," she whispered, voice laced with smoke and honey, "and I will call them back."

The dagger flared brighter, fighting her pull. His knuckles whitened. "I won't swear to you," he ground out, voice low and shaking with effort. "Not now. Not ever."

Camyra's eyes burned hotter, veins of gold threading beneath her skin. "You can't kill me," she hissed. "You *belong* to the fire."

Eldrin's jaw clenched, sweat and blood mixing on his face. "Then I'll burn with it."

Below, through the roar of flame, a voice cut through—hoarse, fierce, defiant.

"Eldrin! Finish her!"

Finnian.

He stood at the base of the burning cage, face streaked with ash, eyes blazing with fury.

Eldrin's grip tightened—but the air thickened, pressing against him like a wall. The dagger trembled, its fire flickering as Camyra's magic coiled tighter around him. She leaned close, her breath ice against his ear. "You can't kill what's already bound to you."

He fought to raise the blade, every muscle shaking, veins standing out along his neck. The mark beneath his tunic burned, answering the dagger's light—but the sorcery held.

"Damn her!" Finnian roared, seizing the rope that held the cage. He braced his boots in the ash, every muscle straining. The cords screamed, fibers splitting one by one.

The cage dropped—inch by inch—toward the inferno below.

"Cover me!" he roared.

For a heartbeat, the light dimmed.

Arrows hissed; steel clashed. Aerion's bow thrummed in rhythm, and Aelar and Caelith drove back the Umbrin pressing too close.

Camyra's eyes snapped toward Finnian. Her lips parted—no words, just a breath that tasted like command.

The black dragon turned midair, smoke spilling from its throat, hatred burning in its eyes.

Death was coming.

"Finnian!" Thalendir shouted, shoving past the melee, sword slick with blood. He pointed upward, voice raw.

"Her dragon—!"

The beast's roar split the sky, flame spilling from its jaws in a torrent.

Finnian didn't stop. He hauled harder; the rope sliced his palms to blood, teeth gritted as the cage groaned lower through the inferno. Sparks stung his skin, heat blistering his face—he could see Eldrin now, framed in firelight, dagger blazing like a star.

Above the roar, another sound cut through—the sharp, familiar beat of wings.

Zeynar burst through the smoke, a shadow edged in silver, his expression fierce and resolute. "Not on my watch!" he shouted, his voice raw over the thunder of flame.

He dove, wings slicing through the haze, twin blades flashing. They crossed the dragon's snout, carving bright trails of sparks—but the creature hardly flinched. With a snarl like cracking stone, the dark beast swung its head, the backdraft of its wings blasting the air apart. One massive claw caught Zeynar mid-flight

He vanished into the firestorm.

"Zeynar!" Aerion's cry broke through the roar—sharp, disbelieving.

A heartbeat later, a shape crashed through the burning canopy, trailing leaves and blood. Zeynar struck the earth hard, his wings folding limply beneath him.

For a moment, no one moved.

Then the dragon reared, flame building in its throat.

Finnian's breath hitched. The ropes screamed as the cage plunged, heat searing his back, shadows clawing close.

"Faster!" Thalendir bellowed, voice raw as he fought to keep the Umbrin from swarming the base.

Above, the dragon drew breath—the air itself recoiling before the roar. Aerion's arrows hissed through the firelight, striking scale only to spark and fall away.

Inside the cage, Eldrin's pulse thundered. The world narrowed to flame and steel. He could feel the dragons' rage in his bones, the mark burning through his chest, the dagger alive in his hand.

Smoke scorched his lungs, ash stung his eyes—but his grip did not falter.

Camyra smiled, eyes bright as molten glass. "Do it," she breathed. "End me… if you can."

"I can," he said, steady as the storm before the strike.

He raised the dagger, light flaring white-hot—

Then the world lurched.

The cage hit the ground with a bone-splintering crash, the shock ripping through his arms. The dagger flew from his grasp, spinning into the ash below, vanishing in the blaze.

Camyra staggered but did not fall. Her laughter cracked through the roar—sharp, breathless, half fury, half triumph.

The ground trembled again. Firelight warped across her face as she turned, golden hair whipping in the heat. "Even fate spares me," she hissed.

Eldrin's glare burned through the haze, his voice a low vow. "Not for long."

The sky burned.

Smoke clawed at Lyria's lungs as she fought for altitude, each wingbeat a battle against the storm. Below, the forest churned in flame; above, the clouds glowed red and gold, mirroring the inferno that hunted her.

Drakor's roar split the heavens.

Lyria twisted hard, wings screaming, the world spinning beneath her. Beside her, Kaelis shouted something lost to the wind—then the shadow fell. Vast, crooked wings blotted out the light. Drakor's scales gleamed like molten obsidian, his breath seething fire between jagged teeth.

Lyria dove.

Flame tore past, close enough to singe her wings. The Shadowcloak flared, its magic buckling under heat and fear, smoke rippling off its edges. For an instant, she vanished—then reappeared in a shimmer of half-light. The mark at her throat pulsed in answer, searing and alive, flooding her with light she could barely contain.

Not yet. Hold.

Kaelis surged alongside her, her cloak flickering wildly, caught between darkness and flame. "We can't outfly him!" she cried, the words whipped apart by the wind.

"You're right," Lyria gasped, forcing her wings wide again, eyes fixed on the chaos below. "Then we outsmart him."

Her mark blazed brighter—silver fire cutting a path through the smoke—and for a heartbeat, even Drakor hesitated. The Shadowcloaks rippled, their magic straining between concealment and defiance, the fabric of shadow twitching with every surge of emotion. They were meant to shield, but in this fury, they burned like mirrors of the soul—barely holding the line between salvation and ruin.

Drakor wheeled high above, circling for the kill. Each beat of his wings thundered through the air. Then—an echoing roar, deeper, colder—rolled up from below.

Lyria's gaze snapped downward. Through layers of smoke, she saw it: the black dragon, still bound to the phantom's will, turning midair—its molten gaze fixed not on her, but on Finnian.

Her pulse seized. "No…"

Kaelis followed her stare, eyes widening. The enslaved dragon dove through the firestorm, smoke spilling from its jaws. Below, amid burning trees, she caught a glimpse of him—hauling the rope, dragging the cage through flame, his skin raw and streaked with blood.

"Finnian!"

"Kaelis—we split!" Lyria shouted, banking hard. "Go after him!"

Kaelis hesitated only a heartbeat before veering away, wings cutting through the haze like silver knives. Her Shadowcloak shimmered wildly, its darkness flaring bright under the surge of fear and fury. Lyria felt the shift in the air—the sudden absence of her friend beside her—and then Drakor's shadow fell.

He came like a storm.

Flame poured from his jaws, the heat blinding. Lyria's mark flared in answer, light bursting across her chest, the Shadowcloak tearing in streaks of black light as its magic fought to keep her hidden. The two forces—light and shadow—warred on her skin, one trying to shield, the other to shine.

The sky split between them—shadow against flame, silver light against the dark.

And below, through the torrent of smoke, the black dragon fell upon Finnian.

Kaelis tucked her wings tight against her back, a snarl curling her lips as she dove. Wind screamed past her ears; the ground rushed up in a whirl of fire and ash. Through the haze, she spotted him—Finnian—darting across the scorched clearing, his hand groping through the debris, searching desperately for the dagger.

The ground shook beneath him.

Flame rippled through the trees, devouring everything in its path. Heat slammed into his back as he stumbled forward, half-blind, lungs burning from smoke and ash.

Finnian's fingers scraped across stone and dirt. Nothing. He shoved aside a charred beam, coughing hard, his skin blistered and bleeding. The dagger had fallen close—he'd seen it, a streak of silver vanishing into the inferno.

"Come on," he rasped, squinting through the haze. "Where are you?"

A gust tore through the clearing, scattering embers like sparks of blood. Then the light shifted—darkened.

Finnian froze.

A shadow blotted out the flames, vast and pulsing. The black dragon descended through the smoke, its wings folding inward, each beat shaking the ground. Its molten eyes locked onto him, blazing with hatred.

His stomach dropped.

Fire licked the ground behind him as the dragon's breath ignited the air. The ground shuddered as the beast landed, claws raking furrows through the earth.

Something glinted ahead—half-buried in ash. The dagger.

Finnian lunged for it. The steel burned cold in his grasp, the light within stuttering like a heartbeat. He scrambled to his feet, breath wild, dagger hilt slick in his palm.

The dragon seethed, its jaws opening, smoke pouring from its throat.

"Finnian!"

Kaelis struck—a flash of silver and fury crashing into the beast's flank. Her blades rang against scale; the dragon roared, twisting violently. Kaelis held on, wings snapping open, her sword carving through the smoke.

He didn't know what the dagger would do. He only knew one thing—if he hesitated, they would all die.

Finnian charged.

Kaelis sliced across the creature's flank again, buying him a breath. "Now!" she screamed.

He didn't hesitate. He dove, shoulder-first, launching himself with the last of his strength. The dragon reared and snapped its jaws down. He drove the dagger up, up between ribs the size of trees—aiming blindly, trusting only the light that thrummed in his veins.

And then—

The same light burst from the Aetherstone at Eldrin's side. And from Lyria's mark, a blaze of flames blazed , as the connection locked.

Eldrin gasped as power flooded through him—through the stone, through the bond, through everything.

Lyria's cry echoed from the sky—bright and fierce—as her light joined his.

The air twisted. The flames bent backward. The three lights fused—burning as one—like a divine spear driving into the black beast, piercing scale and sinew, searing through flesh and bone to the heart beneath as the blade sank home.

Chapter 35

A scream ripped from the dragon—titanic, wrenching, a sound that tore at the air and the earth and every bone in Finnian's chest. Light exploded out along the blade, a white-star flare that raced up his arm and out into the world. The beast convulsed, talons scrabbling, wings thrashing, embers flying like dying stars.

And then Camyra—her shout, a keening note—split the roar. Finnian heard her voice as if from far away: a single syllable, half triumph, half pleading.

He felt it then: a thread—hot, living—snap. The scream transformed; it curved, shrank, became less than a god's howl and more like a mortal thing choking. The dragon's eyes glazed, the molten light dulling in a heartbeat. Its head drooped. With the last of its breath, it exhaled smoke and a small, strangled sound that might have been a name.

Camyra's knees buckled. She slumped as if struck, the black ribbons of rope falling slack across her skin. Her face went white as color drained away. The enchantment that had braided the beast to her unspooled and ripped free.

A surge tore through the Aetherstone at Eldrin's side—then vanished, leaving only cold. He stumbled, breath catching as the light went out. When he looked up, Camyra was already falling.

In the same instant, the life left her—no last speech, no final plea—only a small, shocked silence as she crumpled to the burning earth.

The dragon collapsed after her, a mountain of scorched hide folding in on itself. The ground shuddered under its weight; ash and embers rolled outward in a hot tide.

Finnian staggered back, the dagger heavy in his hand, his heart galloping like a bird trapped in a chest. Blood—his, the beast's, something older—spattered his arms and face. Around him, the battlefield sucked in a breath; cries broke out, then faltered.

Kaelis slid from the dragon's flank and was there at his side in a heartbeat, breath ragged. She dragged him down away from the dying behemoth, one hand beneath his elbow, eyes wide and filled with something like prayer and accusation all at once.

"Finnian—" she whispered, her voice trembling so he couldn't tell if it was outrage or relief.

He looked down at the blade; light slid along its edge, slower now, as if the world itself had finally let go. His hands shook. His chest felt raw and hollow with the sudden absence of noise.

A faint, crooked smile tugged at his mouth.

"I knew you liked me," he murmured.

A pulse of power rippled through the storm—fierce and white and alive.

The mark at Lyria's throat blazed, light flooding her veins, her wings, her soul. For a heartbeat, she felt them both—Eldrin and Finnian—their strength intertwining with hers, three flames bound in one breath.

Her wings snapped open, silver fire streaming, and the Shadowcloak flared in response, its dark weave torn between protection and surrender. Threads of shadow lashed outward, coiling like living smoke, struggling to contain the light surging through her.

The storm bent around her. Drakor faltered mid-flight, eyes narrowing in shock.

Lyria rose, light cutting through the clouds like dawn breaking through ruin.

She dove. Her blade caught the glow of the mark, its edge singing as it carved a white streak across Drakor's shoulder.

He roared, twisting upward, fury and flame bleeding from his maw. Pain turned to hatred, smoke pouring from his nostrils as his wings spread wide, blotting out the firelight.

"You dare!" His voice thundered through the clouds. "You dare strike me with dragon's light!"

Lyria hovered, chest heaving, blade trembling in her grasp. The air around her rippled with heat and raw power. Her Shadowcloak flared again—its magic no longer hiding her, but magnifying her defiance.

"You call yourself dragon," she shouted, voice ringing through the storm, "but you've forgotten what that means!"

Drakor's bellow cracked the air. He surged forward, faster than lightning, claws tearing through the clouds. Lyria banked hard, his tail whipping past, a bolt of black fire that split the sky. The shockwave slammed into her, hurling her sideways, wings shuddering under the strain.

He came again—relentless—breath igniting the heavens, shadow swallowing her light. Each blow rattled her bones; each roar tore at the edges of her mind.

Her mark flickered, dimming beneath the onslaught. The link faltered—the warmth of Eldrin and Finnian slipping away, distance and exhaustion unraveling the thread.

"Fall," Drakor hissed, closing in, his voice like burning stone. "Fall—and I will take the mark!"

He dove, a hurricane of shadow and flame. Lyria twisted, but his wing struck her mid-turn. Pain flared white-hot; she spun out of control, the Shadowcloak shredding around her in ribbons of black light as smoke and blood trailed her fall.

Below, the world roared.

Through the blur of ash, movement rose on the ridge—massive, defiant. Gravorn stood amid the inferno, flame washing over his armored body, eyes burning like forges.

"For the Oath!" his voice boomed, rolling through the firestorm like thunder over stone.

He hurled the boulder.

It tore through the smoke, a mountain set aflame, spinning end over end—until it struck Drakor's side with the force of the world itself.

The dragon convulsed mid-flight, wings flaring wide as scales burst from his chest in a rain of molten shards. His roar shattered the clouds, a sound so violent it seemed to tear the world apart.

Then he fell.

Straight toward Gravorn.

He spiraled from the heavens, fire streaming from his wounds, his body a comet of smoke and flame. The wind of his descent sent Lyria tumbling, heat searing her wings as she fought to stay aloft.

Below, Gravorn did not run.

He planted his feet, shoulders squared, eyes raised, a fist directed at the falling inferno.

Drakor hit the ridge like a cataclysm. The mountain shuddered; fire and stone erupted outward in a blinding wave. Lyria shielded her eyes, the blast hurling her back into the sky.

When the smoke finally began to clear, the ridge was gone—nothing but a blackened scar carved through the mountainside. The dragon lay twisted amid the ruin, the fire around him guttering into ash.

He did not move.

Lyria hovered above the wreckage, trembling. The mark at her throat dimmed to a soft, mournful pulse.

On the shattered ridge, Gravorn was nowhere to be seen.

The wind shifted. The storm quieted. For the first time since the battle began, silence fell over the Arden.

"Gravorn…" she whispered. The word fell like ash from her lips.

And as the smoke curled upward into the dying light, no one heard the faint, buried sound that rumbled beneath the stone—a low, broken growl that trembled through the mountain's heart before fading into silence.

Chapter 36

Finnian stood trembling, the dagger's glow fading in his grasp.

Eldrin lifted his head, dazed but standing, eyes locked on the scar where Drakor had fallen.

"It's done," Finnian breathed.

Ash drifted like snow through the smoke, settling over the ruin in silence.

Lyria touched down where the giant was last seen. The ground was still hot beneath her feet. She pressed a trembling hand to the scorched earth, tears cutting through the soot on her cheeks.

"Rest, stone-heart," she whispered. "You kept your word."

Kaelis landed beside her, wings folding tight against her back. Her voice was hushed, raw. "He saved us."

A sound stirred through the haze—half cough, half growl.

Both turned.

From the wall of smoke and ash, a figure lurched into view—ragged, burned, and impossibly alive. Zeynar. His

Shadowcloak hung in tatters, one wing drooping, his scales dulled and streaked with soot. He pressed an arm to his ribs, every breath a rasp.

"Don't—" he coughed once, grimaced, then managed a grin that was mostly teeth. "—write me off yet."

Lyria blinked, stunned. "Zeynar?"

"Last I checked," he rasped, wings shuddering as he forced them half open. "Though I've had better landings." His gaze swept the collapsing ridge. "The ground's coming down. We have to move."

A deep roar thundered—not the echo of rockfall, but something alive. The mountain *groaned,* veins of molten light cracking through the stone.

Zeynar's grin vanished. "That's not the ground," he hissed.

The tremor rolled beneath their feet, the tunnels shuddering in answer.

"Move!" he barked, louder this time, voice slicing through the din. "Now!"

Lyria turned, forcing her grief into motion. "Gather the wounded! Everyone to the tunnels!"

Aldareth's voice rose over the chaos, hoarse but steady. "Riders! Form up! Guard the flanks!"

Seliora and Erynder emerged through the smoke, rallying what was left of their forces—elves and drelves running shoulder to shoulder toward the ridge. Horses reared, their armor streaked with blood and ash.

Thalendir sprinted ahead, cutting loose the reins of three familiar mounts—Silverwind, Embermane, and Steel. He swung onto Steel's bare back, shouting over the din, "Hurry!"

The ridge shuddered. Stones broke loose, crashing down as the tunnels began to cave, roots writhing in agony, sealing the earth's wounds.

Lyria looked back once. The giants who remained—Gravorn's kin—stood tall amid the smoke, their silhouettes framed in fire. She raised her voice above the storm.

"You kept your oath… The realms will remember!"

One giant—face streaked with ash—pounded his chest in salute. "Go! We'll hold the line," he rumbled.

The mountain roared in answer.

From the tree line, shadows broke loose—sleek, feral shapes with burning eyes. Shadow panthers. They leapt upon the fleeing Umbrin, scattering them in screams and flame. The battlefield erupted once more—dark against dark, chaos devouring itself.

Zeynar shouted. "Faster!"

Wings beat the air. Hooves thundered. The tunnels loomed ahead—pulsing faintly with light, but closing fast.

Lyria turned to Kaelis. "Get them through!"

Kaelis nodded, wings flaring as she flew toward the tunnels, cutting a path through the chaos, urging warriors along. "Go! Keep moving!"

Aldareth's riders surged forward, shields raised as debris rained from above.

Eldrin stood at the rear guard with Finnian, blades flashing in the firelight. When a shadow panther lunged from the smoke, Eldrin met it mid-leap, driving his sword through its chest. The beast collapsed, twitching, and he kicked it aside without slowing.

"Go!" Eldrin shouted, voice raw but commanding. "I'll hold until they're through!"

Finnian turned, firelight glinting across his soot-streaked face. "Not alone, you won't."

The two stood back-to-back for a breath—warriors in the storm—before Eldrin motioned toward the others. "Then we finish this together."

They charged, cutting through the last of the panthers as Aldareth and Thalendir cleared the path. The ridge trembled again, light spilling from cracks beneath their feet.

Only when the final soldiers had vanished into the ground did Lyria and Kaelis follow. The two turned once more toward the blazing ruin behind them.

Zeynar dropped from the air, slamming into the earth as the entrance began to collapse. A shadow panther lunged—

Thwip. Aerion's arrow took it midair.

Zeynar flashed a bloodied grin. "Good shot."

"Jump!" she yelled, grabbing his shoulder.

Together, they dove through the narrowing mouth as the world behind them erupted in light and flame.

The roots sealed. The mountain groaned.

Silence.

And then, faintly—through the stone—a roar rolled from deep beneath the mountain. Distant. It faded into the dark.

The tunnel shook once more, then stilled.

For a long moment, no one spoke. The air hung thick with dust and smoke, their ragged breaths echoing off the stone. Ash drifted from the ceiling in slow spirals; someone coughed, another murmured a prayer. The faint scent of fire still clung to them all — sweat, blood, earth, and loss.

Lyria sank to one knee, pressing a trembling hand against the floor to steady herself. Kaelis stood beside her, chest heaving, eyes fixed on the sealed passage behind them. Aldareth leaned against his horse, his sword tip resting in the dirt. Every sound—the scrape of armor, the shifting of boots—felt too loud in the sudden quiet.

Then—

Eldrin.

He pushed off the wall, staggering once before finding his footing. The Aetherstone at his side flickered weakly, then dimmed to silence. His gaze swept the chamber until it found her.

"Lyria…"

Her name left him as a breath, a prayer. He crossed the space between them, heedless of ash and blood. She looked up as he neared—eyes the same shade of amethyst he'd carried through fire and nightmare—but her expression was calm, uncertain.

"You're alive." His voice cracked, half disbelieving, as he reached for her. "I thought—"

Her hand rose, stopping him before he could touch her. The motion was gentle, not cruel. Her brow furrowed slightly, as though searching his face for something she couldn't find.

"I'm sorry," she whispered. "Do I… know you?"

The words struck harder than any blade.

Eldrin froze, his breath catching in his chest. For a heartbeat, the world seemed to narrow around her face, the silence between them vast and unbearable. Then he forced a faint smile, though his voice trembled. "It's me. Eldrin. You—" The words broke apart.

Her gaze softened, but confusion clouded it. "I don't know you," she said quietly. "Step back."

Eldrin's jaw went slack. He turned to Kaelis, searching her face for denial, for hope.

Kaelis turned away, eyes burning. She knew now what memory the Tree Sage had taken.

Finnian stood nearby, his expression carved in disbelief. No one spoke.

Eldrin lowered his hand slowly, the hollow thrum of the Aetherstone echoing in his chest. He swallowed hard. "You don't remember me?" The words scraped raw, barely sound.

Lyria's gaze drifted past him, distant and searching, as though hearing something far away. "No…" she murmured. "Should I?"

The silence stretched—fragile as glass, heavy as loss.

Kaelis wiped the mist from her eyes. As much as she disliked the thought of Lyria with him, she hated this even more. It was cruel beyond belief. She turned to Finnian first, trying to explain with her eyes. But none came.

Eldrin met her gaze. She glanced down, unable to hold it, a lump forming in her throat.

"Explain…" Eldrin said quietly. "What is going on?"

All eyes turned to Kaelis. She shifted from one foot to the other, her throat working before she finally stepped closer, placing a steadying hand on Lyria's arm.

"This is Eldrin," she began softly. "He's your friend. He saved your life—and you risked yours for him. He's the reason we came to the Arden… the reason we fought through flame and shadow."

Her voice faltered, barely audible as she added, "You came to free him."

Lyria stared at her friend. Then, at the elf standing before her—the one with the green eyes. She didn't move or breathe, only stood there, searching his face as if memory might rise from the ashes if she just looked hard enough.

Kaelis swallowed, her voice trembling. "I think…" She hesitated, glancing between them, her throat tightening around the words. "I think you loved him."

Lyria's brow furrowed, her wings twitching faintly beneath the ash. "Love?" she echoed, as if testing the word for meaning. A small, incredulous laugh escaped her. "Me… in love with an elf?"

Kaelis managed a faint smile that didn't reach her eyes. "I know it sounds impossible. But you risked all our lives for him. That has to mean something."

"I don't even remember him," Lyria said, her voice cracking on the edge of frustration. "How could I love him?"

The silence that followed was heavy enough to crush breath.

Eldrin's throat tightened, but he didn't speak. His fingers brushed the Aetherstone at his side, feeling its faint pulse echo the hollow rhythm of his heart.

The quiet pressed closer — thick, unyielding — until Finnian finally cleared his throat. "Well," he said, forcing a wry grin that didn't quite reach his eyes, "that's one way to make a fellow feel invisible."

No one spoke. They just looked at one another — uneasy, uncertain, caught between relief and grief with no words to bridge it.

"How did this happen?" Eldrin asked at last, his voice rough. "Why doesn't she know who I am?"

His gaze found Kaelis — sharp, searching, desperate for an answer.

She stepped forward, wings drooping, ears twitching as she struggled to find the right words. Lyria tilted her head, curiosity flickering. Whatever Kaelis was about to say, she wanted to hear it.

"It was her choice," Kaelis said quietly. "To sacrifice a memory to the Tree Sage in return for the tunnels opening — to free you. She didn't get to choose which memory he took." Her voice faltered, breaking on the last words. "It was ripped from her."

Eldrin stumbled back a step, breath coming ragged as the truth settled like stone in his chest. She had given up *him* — their bond, their fight, their promise — so that he might live.

Lyria watched him, confusion shadowing her eyes. She saw the pain in his face but didn't understand its shape — couldn't name it.

"Why are you looking at me like that?" she whispered.

Eldrin tried to speak, but the words caught, breaking against the silence that filled the space between them.

Finnian spoke first. "Because," he muttered, voice rough, "he loved you too."

The air hung heavy again, thick with what none of them could say.

Somewhere far above, the mountain groaned, the faintest tremor running through the stone — as if the world itself mourned what had been lost.

Chapter 37

Eldrin ached from head to toe — from battle, from captivity, from every blow the night had dealt him.

But his heart ached more.

The thought of Lyria not remembering him hurt worse than any wound he carried.

Dust hung in the air, trembling in the faint light filtering through cracks above. Around him, the survivors moved in silence — tending wounds, whispering prayers — yet their voices felt far away.

All Eldrin could hear was the echo of her words: *Do I know you?*

He looked at Lyria again. Studied her.

She stood beside Kaelis — steady, composed, and utterly unfamiliar. She was alive. Whole.

And yet, she didn't know him.

For a long moment, he only watched. The ache in his chest deepened — then slowly hardened into resolve. "You may have forgotten me," he murmured, "but I'll make you remember — everything we fought for."

Finnian stepped beside him, limping slightly, twin blades strapped across his back. "You're not giving up, are you?"

Eldrin shook his head once. "I can't." His breath hitched as he added, softer, "I love her."

Finnian glanced down — the dagger still rested in his grip, its edge dulled with ash but faintly glowing beneath the grime. For a heartbeat, it pulsed — alive.

He turned it over, then extended it toward Eldrin, hilt first. "Then you're going to need this."

Their eyes met — exhaustion, friendship, and something like hope passing between them.

Eldrin's fingers closed around the hilt. The moment he touched it, the Aetherstone at his side flickered in answer — a whisper of white light, fragile but unbroken.

For a moment, neither spoke.

Then Eldrin murmured, "Thank you."

Finnian managed a half-smile — tired, uneven, but genuine. "Anytime. But next time, let's skip the part where you nearly get killed."

A weak laugh escaped Eldrin. "Deal."

Finnian turned away — and something in the air shifted.

The torchlight flickered once, dimmed, then brightened again, as if breathing.

The dagger's glow pulsed faintly in Eldrin's grasp — and when Finnian turned back, Eldrin froze.

Two mirrored lines of light shimmered just beneath Finnian's temples — faint at first, then steady.

Like reflections of the dagger's fire — but alive, pulsing with their own rhythm.

For a heartbeat, everyone held still.

Silence rippled through the tunnel as the others turned.

Lyria's mark flared in answer, soft silver gleaming at her throat.

The Aetherstone at Eldrin's side hummed in quiet resonance.

Even the torches seemed to bow to the moment.

"What?" Finnian frowned, looking around.

Eldrin took a step closer, disbelief softening into awe.

"It's you…" He whispered.

Then — from somewhere deep within the stone — a whisper unfurled, soft and ancient, threading through shadow and breath alike:

The second mark has awakened.

The torches guttered.

And in the breath between light and dark, the world seemed to hold its breath—

Then darkness took them.

The prophecy stirs again…

Continue the adventure in the Elves, Drelves & Dragons series:

Book Three — Cry of Dragons

ELVES, DRELVES & DRAGONS
BOOK 3
CRY OF DRAGONS
C. STAR

If you enjoyed this book, please take a moment to write a review.

It will help others find my books (so I can keep writing in this series).

Thanks for your review!

C. Star

Character & Creature Guide

Main Characters

- **Lyria Ironwing** ***(LEER-ee-uh)*** — Drelf mark-bearer, part dragon, part elf.
- **Eldrin** ***(ELL-drin)*** — Elven warrior, son of King Eldermyst.
- **Finnian** ***(FIN-ee-an)*** — Elf. Eldrin's loyal friend.
- **Gantar** ***(GAN-tar)*** — Elven sage and healer.
- **Thalendir** ***(THAL-en-deer)*** — Elf. Eldrin's older brother, son of King Eldermyst.
- **King Eldermyst** ***(ELL-der-mist)*** — King of the Elves, father to Eldrin and Thalendir.
- **Kaelis Skythorn (KAY-liss SKY-thorn)** — Drelf. Lyria's fiercely loyal best friend from the Drelf Kingdom.
- **Orendir** ***(OR-en-deer)*** — Elf. High Warden to King Eldermyst.
- **Nyxari the Veilkeeper (NICK-sar-ee) —** Drelf seer who interprets visions of fate and prophecy. Keeper of ancient lore tied to the marks.
- **Seralyth** ***(SERR-uh-lith)*** — Ancient white dragon.
- **Thariel** ***(THAR-ee-el)*** — Elf. Eldrin's mother.
- **Fizzlewing** ***(FIZZ-uhl-wing)*** — Mischievous pixie guide from the Shrouded Vale.

Elven Council

- **Lady Alariel** ***(AH-lar-ee-el)*** — Mistress of Lore.
- **Lord Thalion** ***(THAL-ee-on)*** — Commander of the Elven Guard.
- **Elder Faelorn** ***(FAY-lorn)*** — Master of Nature.
- **Lady Seraphina** ***(SERR-uh-fee-nuh)*** — Ambassador of Alliances.
- **Elder Sylthir** ***(SILL-theer)*** — The Shadow Watcher.

Horses

- **Silverwind** ***(SILL-ver-wind)*** — Eldrin's mare.
- **Duskrunner** ***(DUSS-kruhn-er)*** — Gantar's gelding, ridden by Lyria.
- **Embermane** ***(EM-ber-mayn)*** — Finnian's buckskin gelding.
- **Steel** ***(STEEL)*** — Thalendir's black stallion.

Creatures

- **Nemods (NEH-mods)** — Abyss-born horrors of shadow and flame. Their cracked hides glow with molten veins, their ember eyes burning with soulless hunger. Once bound to dragon kind, they now serve Vartharax and his lieutenant, Drakor.

- **Wyverns (WHY-vernz)** — Winged, reptilian beasts smaller than dragons but no less fierce.
- **Shadowmanes (SHAD-oh-mayns)** — Nightmarish steeds forged of shadow and fire, ridden by nemods into battle. Their blackened hides cling to skeletal frames, hooves carving scorched trenches as they ride. Eyes burning like molten glass, their silent gallop carries the echo of nightmares through the dark.
- **Shadow Panthers (SHA-doh PAN-thurz).** — Stealth-born predators woven of smoke and sinew. Once forest guardians, they were corrupted by Vartharax's darkness. Their eyes burn amber-red, their claws cut like obsidian, and when slain—after several strikes, for they move through both flesh and spirit—they dissolve into mist, leaving only silence and ash behind.
- **Aetherstone (AY-ther-stone)** — An ancient relic of power, said to guide its bearer when all light is lost.
- **Gladehorn (GLAYD-horn)** — Watcher of Balance in the drelf realm. A reindeer-like guardian with silver-dappled fur, spiraled antlers that glow at dusk, and calm, water-clear eyes.
- **Skitterling (SKI-tur-ling)** — Small, swift creatures with foxlike faces and green-gold hides feathered along their wings and tails. Once used by dragons as

spies and decoys, they were nearly hunted to extinction by their own masters.

- **Gravorn (GRAH-vorn)** — A giant and ally to the drelves. Stoic and bound by oath, he aids Lyria's war-band in the battle against Drakor, embodying ancient strength and loyalty.
- **Tree Sage** — Ancient, sentient spirit of the Arden's roots who aids Lyria and her allies by opening hidden paths.

Dragons

- **Zyressa (ZAI-ress-uh)** — A fierce green dragon, scarred by battle and quick to challenge those who cross her.
- **Korrath (KOR-ath)** — A crimson dragon of immense power and pride, longtime rival of Drakor.
- **Drakor (DRAY-kor)** — Twisted lieutenant of Vartharax. Smaller than most of his kind but more cunning, he wields shadow and deceit as weapons.
- **Vartharax (VAR-thuh-raks)** — The Dark Dragon Lord who broke the ancient Covenant and commands the nemods.
- **Velthar (VELL-thar)** — A rogue bronze-scaled dragon who conspires with Zyressa for his own gain.

- **Rhaegorath (RAY-goh-rath)** — The black dragon bound to Camyra's will, summoned through dark magic to serve her command.

More Elves

- **Master Trainer Aldareth (AL-dah-reth) —** Veteran weapons master of the Elven Guard and mentor to Eldrin. In Book Two, he leads the spies that Gantar sends into the Arden.
- **Caelith (KAY-lith) —** Skilled elven warrior who trains and patrols with Eldrin in Book One. In Book Two, he serves as one of Gantar's spies under Aldareth's command.
- **Aelar (AY-lar) —** Quiet, sharp-eyed spy sent by Gantar to accompany Aldareth on the mission into the Arden.
- **Dareth (DARE-eth) —** Scout who patrolled the Elven borders in Book One and fought to protect the realm's outer forests.
- **Erynder (AIR-in-der) —** Veteran Elven scout who fought beside King Eldermyst to defend the drelf kingdom. In Book Two, he remains behind to aid the drelves, joining Lyria's war-band and scouting the Umbrin alongside Seliora.
- **Aerion (EYE-ree-on)** — Calm and precise female elven archer, unmatched with a bow. In Book Two,

she serves among Gantar's spies sent with Master Aldareth into the Arden.

- **Seliora (Seh-lee-OR-ah) —** Red-haired, emerald-eyed female elf who fought beside King Eldermyst to defend the drelf kingdom. Remaining behind to aid the drelves, she later joins Lyria's war-band, scouting the Umbrin alongside Erynder before the battle.

Dark Elves/Umbrin/Nightborn

- **Drovane (DROH-vayn) —** Leader of the Umbrin, the dark elves. His serpent-smooth voice and black eyes conceal centuries of ambition and deceit.
- **Camyra (KAH-mih-rah) —** The golden-haired enchantress aligned with the dark elves. Her allure masks a dangerous will; she commands the black dragon Rhaegorath through forbidden magic.

More Drelves

Zeynar (ZAY-nar) — Drelf warrior sent by Nyxari to guide Master Trainer Aldareth and the Elven spies through the Arden to the Umbrin camp.

About the Author

C. Star grew up in rural Nebraska, the youngest of three and the only girl—taunted and teased by her older brothers, which she's convinced made her fierce, determined, and full of stories worth telling.

She wrote her first book at ten years old and hasn't stopped since. From early stories scribbled in notebooks to award-winning song lyrics written on a whim, storytelling has always been in her bones.

After writing in other genres under the name Cynthia Star, she followed her heart into young adult fantasy—where magic awakens, dragons rise, and unlikely heroes dare to change the world.

C. Star now lives in New Mexico, where she hikes the desert foothills with her dog, River, collects odd-shaped rocks, and dreams up new worlds with every step.

You can check out all my books on Amazon by Cynthia Star

(know a young person who likes dragons?)

The Beepy Bumpy Blue Bug ~ picture book (ages 2-6)

What Color is Your Dragon? ~ picture book (ages 4-8)

The Moonlit Dragon ~ picture book (ages 4-8)

The Dragon Flyers Book One ~ (ages 7-10)

The Dragon Flyers Book Two ~ (ages 7-10)

The Dragon Flyers Book Three ~ (ages 7-13)

The Dragon Flyers Book Four ~ (ages 8-13)

Happiness Came with a Cat (New Edition) ~ Adult memoir/self-help

#1 Amazon Best Seller - Starving, Bingeing, Purging ~ Adult memoir/self-help

www.ingramcontent.com/pod-product-compliance
Lightning Source LLC
LaVergne TN
LVHW020536100826
845148LV00010B/1481

* 9 7 9 8 9 8 5 0 6 8 1 9 1 *